SANGUINARY LONGINGS

CLAUDE FRAZIER

Peter Birchinall FASI. BH.

Scintillation Books

Part One

FRANCE, 1918

Cole lay his hand on the shoulder of the dirty young private leaning against one of the tent supports. Startled out of his fatigued reverie, he uttered a sleepy, "Sir?"

"I need you to put that soldier on the operating table," he said, pointing to a bloody bundle on the ground just outside the tent.

Cole watched the boy, whose wounds he had dressed less than an hour ago, pick up the unconscious man and position him so that he and another private with minor wounds could strip the smelly, torn clothing from the next surgical case.

Cole doubted the man would survive the amputation of his gangrenous leg but he would do what he could to save his life.

The sleepy private had the man's pants half off when he looked up suddenly and seemed to Cole to have an incredulous look on his face when he lurched backwards as his forehead exploded. The crack of the rifle came a grace note before a deafening stream of popping, not unlike over-sized hail on a tin roof.

Cole turned towards the attack and saw the first German less than 10 yards away. Cole ran for his sidearm dangling from a small hook on a tent pole.

As the lead German ran under the edge of the tent, he lunged at Cole with the long bayonet of his rifle. The blade plunged through Cole's left hand as he used his right to claw his pistol from its holster. Somehow Cole fired, striking the soldier in the neck.

The German collapsed, puling Cole down with the impaled hand. As Cole writhed with pain, a harsh kick in the ribs brought him to a breathless stillness. As his vision cleared, he saw a German officer smirking over him. The man said in nearly perfect English, "Your patients are not needing you, and we have no need of you either—so I must bid you goodbye."

Cole's body rocked with the force of the bullet to his chest. *The bastard shot me,* he thought, as he lost consciousness.

Cole's sister scolded him. She punched on his chest and screeched, "Get up and play with me—you said you would, now get up!" She pounded on his chest some more and somehow on his back as well. Lilly was gone now, but the aching in his chest and back continued, a rhythmic pulse that ran through his thorax.

An especially painful jolt brought Cole some aware-ness of his surroundings, icy cold, bouncing along, lying in the back of a creaking, shuddering wooden cart. Other people, or corpses, rocked against him as the cart struggled down a pitted, rugged path. Numerous rocks encumbered the passage of this conveyance to its destination. When the wheels struck larger rocks the pain was so intense that Cole feared it was part of the final drop into Hell.

As Cole began to slip into the cold forever, he pulled back from the sleep he wanted to embrace when he heard voices and saw moving lights through his closed eyelids. He could not call out or move, and he did not really feel the hands that lifted him from the cart and brought him into a place where warm air struck his face. Cole heard a booming, lilting voice say, "Move this one to the moribund room. He is too wan, barely breathing."

Cole started again; he must have lost consciousness for a while. He sensed he was in a new room, darker, quieter, a heavy oppressive stillness of the air. Someone had placed him on his side. He could open his eyes now. The lights seemed to flicker but he had a wavering vision of two young women in maids' dress bending over an ivory statue and a young man directing tubes from each of his arms into scarlet splattered glass vessels on the floor.

How odd. I did not know statues could bleed, he thought, as he fell into sleep.

"So, this is the young captain, the doctor? How pale and how handsome," Madame Cailletet said.

"Shall we speed him along, Madame," whispered her first maid.

Cole opened his eyes and stared into Madame Cailletet's icy blue eyes.

She started. "Excuse me, Sir, I did not know you were awake."

Cole continued to stare at Madame Cailletet. He was too weak to speak. He maintained his focus on Madame Cailletet's eyes until his eyelids fluttered and closed.

Madame Cailletet continued to examine Cole's face and asked the medical orderly about his injuries and his identity.

"We will return soon. When we do, we will relieve you for a while," she said.

True to her word, Madame Cailletet swept into the desolate little room less than an hour later with her first and second maids in train. The bedraggled orderly allowed himself to be taken into the care of Madame Cailletet's comely second maid for a trip to the warm kitchen for hot coffee, soup, and bread. Madame Cailletet and her first maid, Bridgett, took full responsibility for the orderly's doomed charges.

"Bolt the door, Bridgett."

"Yes, Madame."

Her mistress sat at a rickety writing desk in a dusty corner and laid out a clean cloth on which she rested her arm. Bridgett removed a hypodermic needle and a syringe from a small box tucked in her apron pocket.

Bridgett expertly inserted the needle into Madame Cailletet 's vein and withdrew a syringe full of blood. A plaster was positioned on Madame Cailletet's arm and Bridgett quickly moved to Cole's bed and deftly inserted the needle of the syringe into Cole's right arm. She withdrew a little of his blood to convince herself that the needle was in Cole's vein, and then she slowly injected her mistress's blood into Cole.

Cole swore and tried to move but Bridgett held his arm firmly as she finished the transfer of Madame Cailletet's blood.

Bridgett applied a plaster onto Cole's arm and returned the syringe to its wooden storage box.

Madame Cailletet had gotten up and brushed Cole's black hair from his moist forehead.

"Check the other two soldiers, Bridgett while I try to give him a sip of water."

The two women sat with the three men for a while, unbolted the door, and prepared to go up to the kitchen to send the, undoubtedly, most grateful orderly back to his charges.

Before they left the smelly little room, Madame Cailletet told Bridgett, "Move him to a ward tomorrow and send a barber to cut his hair."

Both women smiled in anticipation of the morning miracle and left the room that now sheltered only two dying men.

A feeble light from the room's puny high-set windows awoke Cole shortly after dawn. He did not know where he was, rising and falling back onto the cot, feeling the rough, sweat-soaked sheets beneath him. He cried out from the sharpness of the pain which seemed to come from everywhere but especially his chest. He tried not to move while the pain became manageable. He had to force himself to breathe when he realized he was holding his breath from fear of movement of his chest.

Eventually, he had control of his breathing and the white-hot intensity of the pain stabbing at him from a dozen points began to fade enough that he could begin to think and to open his eyes.

"Where the Hell am I," he muttered.

"Bloody poor accommodation it is, young sir, but not quite Hell," said Sergeant Miller. "Considering how you were last night and, no offense to the saintly young man that you no doubt be, I should think you should be most grateful to higher power that you are not reading the inscription at the gate to Hades right now."

Cole slowly turned his face to look at the visage of the visitor. A weather worn, lined face with a carefully trimmed pencil mustache was the source of the voice and this less than friendly looking countenance now seemed to be making a full attempt at a smile for Cole's benefit.

"The truth be, you are in a nice, and I might add beautiful lady's splendid country house. The French, English, and now the Americans let her help with injured soldiers. The locals found you last evening, the lone survivor of the villainous attack on your field hospital. They could only take you here. We normally do not get injured here who need a surgeon, but the same ignoble band who attacked you also found the time to slaughter all but two in a nearby American patrol.

"In point of fact, they did kill the entire patrol since those brave young men died last night. As you should have done. A most marvelous miracle. We deal mostly with the mind here, not the body. I have nothing much to offer you, but here you lie before my humble self this fine morning. We dare not move you. We have sent to the Americans for a doctor to examine you. They will work out what to do next."

"I need water and I'm hungry," said Cole in a raspy, low voice.

"I have dealt with many injured over the years. I would rather not give you anything until the doctor sees you, but your chest wound seems quiet, and I don't think your gut is injured. I will tell the maids to look to you and try a bit of water and soup."

Sergeant Miller turned away but stopped and faced Cole again. "I will be most grateful, young sir, if you would recover heartily. The mistress of the house is attached to you already, and I would hate to see her hurt by your dwindling away."

"I will do my best to not disappoint you, Sergeant," grunted Cole.

"Oh, one more thing. Who the Hell are you? You had nothing with you. We were just told you appeared to be an American field surgeon."

"I am Captain Cole Sterling."

"Indeed you are, Sir. And I will so inform the beneficent lady of the house," said the Sergeant as he walked from the room as Cole closed his eyes and slept.

"Captain, please eat something now," said the young provincial French woman.

Cole had been raised to a near sitting position, his back braced with firm pillows. He was perplexed at how little he hurt and even more surprised that he was hungry.

He focused on the soup, a hearty country soup, and the tough chewy bread. Occasional sips of cool water with a strong mineral taste allowed him to get the bread down.

"I thought I saw you last night with one of the soldiers who died. It looked like he had colored streams falling from his body," said Cole

"You were very sick last night, feverish. We cleaned and rebandaged the soldier. There were no colored streams.Unless death wears them when he comes to call," said the girl.

"What is your name?"

"I am Colette. I am Madame Cailletet's second maid."

"Sergeant Miller told me the Americans would send someone to see me. Are they nearby?"

"I do not know. There is heavy fighting. We hear cannon much of the day. They may not come for a while," said Colette.

Can I move from this room? I would like to see the sun's light and anything but these walls."

"We are afraid you will bleed again if we move you," said Colette.

"I am better. You can move me slowly, carefully. I will hold my breath, but not too long."

"You are a doctor, so I am told, you should not joke about such things. You could be closer to the edge than you know," Colette said with the solemnity that her position as second maid required. She maintained the crease in her brow but said, "I will notify Madame and the Sergeant of your wishes." Colette stood and took his food tray from the room, scowling so intensely that it seemed comically theatrical.

Colette had left Cole propped up and he examined the dark little room. He felt for the two young soldiers. What a horrible place to die. He selfishly missed their presence. To hear another American's voice here would have been a breath of home. Maybe Colette was correct. Perhaps he was too sure of recovery.

With a small bump going from the cot to the stretcher, he could hemorrhage and no one there could possibly help him. He could exit this moldy room not a rejuvenated gallant hero but a pitiful, bloody, mangled corpse in a shroud.

Cole gloomily assessed his circumstances and struggled to fight panic. He heard footsteps from the stairs and was elated to see Madame Cailletet enter the narrow doorway. Her hair was down now and she wore a delicate white blouse and black fashionable dress. The beautiful lady before him bore little resemblance to the stern woman he had seen yesterday.

"Do you remember me, Captain Sterling?"

"Yes, but at the time your face seemed indistinct, behind distorted glass. My poor vision did not reveal your beauty to me."

Madame Cailletet blushed but said, "Captain, you could not see because you were dying. Now you are not. I intended to let you recover a little more before moving you upstairs, but Colette told me of your surprising strength. I will have you moved immediately to less distasteful surroundings."

Cole said, "How could you think I was dying and only a few hours later, I am safely recovering?"

"I will explain upstairs. The servants will open the drapes a little in your new room. Your eyes will be sensitive so be careful in viewing our country garden outside. Observing birds and flowers in a sunlit garden is a blessing from God. We never know when such a blessing can be taken from us, Captain Sterling."

Cole stared at Madame Cailletet as she walked away.

"Maybe I have died and Hell is a lunatic asylum. I am dying, then I am not, and please watch the flora and fauna here in France, good Captain."

Before Cole's bewilderment grew too profound, two husky men brought a stretcher and with no great regard for his person or his pain, moved and galumphed him from the little dungeon, up a collection of steps to a wonderfully appointed room with the promised garden window. Actually, there were three large windows and all had heavy drapes suggestively parted.

Cole's pain was so all-consuming that he was only vaguely aware of the room or the bed on which he was positioned, but such was the power of Madame Cailletet's suggestion that even fighting to not wretch on her fine bed linen, he gazed at the glorious light streaming from the window. He had never seen such light. His eyes teared and he struggled upright as he tried to leave the bed. His legs dangled from the bedside, his hands pushed against the mattress and he fell backward in a faint as soon as his haunches left the soft silk beneath his skin.

~

Cole stirred under the bed covers and felt someone adjust his pillow.

"It is unnerving to never know when I will wake up or who will be there," Cole said.

A pretty young woman said, "At least you woke up, not far from here, many do not. I am Bridgett. Madame Cailletet's first maid. I bathed you and dressed your wounds while you were asleep. We first thought you were dead, but then you snored. Most men would have found my bathing them a most delightful experience, but you only snored like a great pig. But men are pigs, so I am not surprised."

Cole turned his head toward the windows. Now only a dim light shone through the curtains. Bridgett saw his gaze and said, "Yes, Madame wants you to view the garden." She pushed a wheel chair to Cole's bed. The chair was rickety and appeared to date from the Napoleonic Wars.

"Don't worry, the chair will hold your scrawny backside," she said.

Bridgett was surprising strong and deftly maneuvered him from the bed to the chair, and now Cole peered out at Madame Cailletet's garden.

The twilight did not hurt his eyes at first, and he peered out at the carefully sculpted garden of statues and hedges, decorative pools, roses and late season flowers.

Birds busied themselves seeking worms. Cole saw Madame Cailletet, or so he thought, in her garden. Curiously, she was completely covered; gloves, broad brimmed hat, scarves and dark glasses made her an odd figure in the mild early autumn weather.

"The garden is beautiful but there must be something wrong with my eyes. The light seems to be intensifying and my eyes are tearing again," said Cole.

"We will get you glasses like Madame," Bridgett said.

"I am sure I will be fine tomorrow. My eyes were probably irritated somehow while I was unconscious."

Bridgett left his chair near a settee with a mahogany side table. She wound a phonograph on the table and Mozart prodded him to release his dark thoughts as the sun faded out behind the heavy curtains.

The mechanism in the phonograph was powerful and Mozart was still soaring when he went to sleep, lolling against the arm of the sad old chair.

A great thump startled Cole awake. Bridgett positioned a polished square at Cole's elbow, then raised and lowered two sidepieces to create an adequate dining surface for two people.

An elderly woman he had not seen before set the table and left behind a few covered dishes and a darkly-tinted crystal decanter. The two women scurried out without a word when Madame came in and stood at his side.

To Cole, Madame Cailletet seemed more beautiful with each encounter. Her hair was radiant in the candlelit room. Her eyes and her diamond earrings sparkled. He made a feeble effort to rise, but Madame softly pressed his shoulder to keep him seated.

"Will you join me, Captain, in a light supper," she asked.

"I can think of nothing I would enjoy more, but my appetite may not be equal to my delight in your company," said Cole.

"You do know how to charm, Captain," Madame Cailletet laughed. "Sergeant Miller said he believed you to be an American from the South and gentleman soldiers from there are reputedly great scoundrels and silver -tongued beguilers of women."

"Sergeant Miller probably has a fondness for romantic novels concerning the American Civil War. I doubt I can meet his expectations," replied Cole.

Madame Cailletet poured some water for Cole and gave him small servings of a medley of vegetables and a small portion of pan-fried trout. Cole had not been presented with food like this in weeks but he noticed that Cailletet picked at the vegetables and ignored the fish. Cole complimented the table she had sat before him but Madame Cailletet seemed distracted

"I should tell you the maids struggle with your French. They say your speech is, well, a vulgar word they learned from the English enlisted men. I find your accent execrable but overall you complete your sentences well and you certainly understand us nicely. Where did you learn your French?" asked Madame Cailletet.

"My mother taught French in a finishing school before marrying my father. She taught me at an early age. She had a difficult relationship with my father and we often spoke French between us. My father rightly thought it was conspiratorial. My mother did not have the opportunity of studying in France or my accent might meet your approval. My mother was delighted that I would visit France when she could not until she realized that the Germans shoot at doctors, too."

"You said your mother had a difficult relationship with your father. Is he dead?" asked Madame Cailletet.

"Yes, he died when I was a young teen. He was very critical of me. He intended me to be in business with him and was trying to mold me in his image, a process that was not going well at the time of his passing. Nonetheless, I like to believe that he would have eventually understood that I was meant for a different life.," said Cole.

"Bridgett said you have neither a wife or fiancee."

"That is correct," said Cole.

"I hope I am not too intrusive—you should not think all French women are nosy," said Madame Cailletet.

Cole laughed. "My experience in the parlors of Mississippi and Massachusetts is that ladies are always interested in their visitor's family."

Madame did not smile with Cole.

"My questioning is not ideal female chatter, Captain.

I need to know your circumstances before I tell you how and why your life here has been changed for all time."

"Now you have my attention," said Cole quietly.

"Have you speculated on your miraculous recovery without benefit of a fellow surgeon," said Madame Cailletet.

"Yes, your maids have up to now prevented me from getting a good view of my chest wound. Now that I am better I will examine the site tomorrow. I speculate that the bullet may not have lodged but bounced off a rib, but led to a fair amount of blood loss."

"What became of the bullet I cannot say, but you were mortally wounded, drained of blood and near death. You had hours to live when I gave you some of my blood in a syringe."

"American military doctors are performing experimental transfusions, but you could not have given me enough of your blood to make a difference and I could have died from a reaction to your blood," Cole said with marked incredulity.

"You don't understand; I was not replacing lost blood. I was transforming you. Making you like me. I am never sick. I am nearly 50 but I barely appear 30. I see as well in the dark as others do in the day, and I am incredibly strong."

Cole now stared at Madame Cailletet with a mixture of amazement and revulsion.

Madame Cailletet stood and said softly, "I know it seems mad. You will believe soon enough."

She walked to the door and said, "Good night,

Captain. In the morning avoid the light. It will burn your eyes and your skin."

The elderly woman soon approached, cleared the table and pushed it out of Cole's path to his bed. Cole longed to plunge under the bed covers, but crept in the wheelchair to a full-length dressing mirror near the bed's headboard. He opened his robe and began to strip away the plasters on his chest. He gasped when he saw what had been a draining mess was now a closed wound with a bright red scar.

After a while, he closed the robe over his chest and rolled the wheel chair to the opposite wall near an ornate antique rocking chair. He pulled himself up and slid onto the cushion seat of the chair, where he rocked slowly. He heard the house quieting and going to sleep around him.

Cole tried to consider what he had been told and what he had seen, but his mind was foggy and his emotions flooded through his thoughts. A surgeon cannot be confined to the dark. He had put his personal life aside during his long demanding training but he longed for a woman to complete him, to make him a home, to have his children. If he really believed this insanity, all the life he had imagined before him was swept away from him as if he were an insect being swept away by a flood.

Cole left the chair and walked to the curtains. He thrust them aside, flooding the dark room with silvery light from a full moon. Madame's garden was now more vivid than when seen at twilight. The plants seemed to shine, the statues glowed, and he saw in detail the garden rabbits, mice, and a stealthy fox that was closing in on an unsuspecting rabbit. The fox grasped the squealing rabbit by its throat and the reddest blood Cole had ever seen showered over the plants.

The blood fixated Cole. The crunching of the fox on the limp corpse repulsed him, but the blood seemed alive and filled Cole with an unfamiliar longing. He paced the room for a few times then hurried to seek an outside door.

He stumbled and lurched downstairs, soon finding a door that led to a terrace overlooking the garden. The cool outside air stimulated Cole as he looked for the steps. He started when a voice emanated from the opposite end of the terrace.

"Captain, I thought you might venture outside," said Madame Cailletet.

She went to him, took his hand, and led him off the terrace. They found the site of the little rabbit's demise. The fox had carried the carcass to a safer location to savor his meal. Wisps of fur were beside a small patch of blood soaked earth. The droplets of blood scattered about the foliage still enticed Cole.

Madame Cailletet asked, "Do you smell the blood?"

Cole nodded yes.

"Animal blood has a different odor than human blood. A bull's blood is as different from this tiny creature as ours from the bull's." She did not let him linger, pulling him out of the cultivated setting and into the forest.

At first walking was easy. The gardeners kept the brush cut back near the lawn, but soon the forest was natural and they had to dodge fallen trees and dense clusters of low growth among the solemn maples and oaks.

Moonlight filtered through the trees dimly but Cole could see well and had no trouble avoiding obstacles. Madame Cailletet held his hand firmly. He wondered if she thought he might bolt, but in truth, he was comforted by her presence and oddly serene.

They walked at a brisk pace, weaving among the trees, until they came to a vigorous stream with large rocks scattered about the bank and within the water. Madame Cailletet removed her shoes. Cole looked down and realized he had thin slippers on his feet and a light robe as his only clothing.

Madame Cailletet laughed. "Take those ridiculous slippers off, but you might want to adjust that robe. There is a chill in the air and it must be a bit breezy since you don't have anything under the robe."

Cole blushed and tightened his robe around him. Madame Cailletet drew Cole out into the stream, hopping from rock to rock. She never released his hand and managed to bring them to a small outcropping near the middle of the stream. There they sat and watched the moon traverse the sky, stars blinking among the clouds.

As unquiet as Cole's mind had been an hour ago, he now was in a separate place and at peace. He knew this would not last but welcomed the tranquility.

After a long while, Madame Cailletet released his hand and stretched out on her side, facing Cole, her head resting on the palm of her hand.

"I don't know why we are different and why our blood is transformative," said Madame Cailletet. "At least sometimes," she added with a tone that Cole thought was melancholic. She cleared her throat and went on. "My grandfather changed me when I was 16. I was out riding, near here, actually. My horse was startled and threw me. I was bleeding internally and was near death when he did it for me, although more primitively than what I did for you. "

"I soon recovered but suffered the same affliction as my grandfather, who was locally believed to be slightly mad and notoriously reclusive. He gave me guidance on how to survive, but never told me the origins of his condition, probably because I was 16, and especially in those days, he may have thought that I should not be told things that, in his mind, were not for a young girl's ears.

"Before my 17th birthday, he died while out on a visit to his mistress in a nearby town. His head was nearly severed by what was probably a cavalryman's sword. Officially, his death was a robbery, but all believed he had been killed by his mistress's husband, a cavalry colonel.

"He had an arranged alibi among his comrades and no one wanted to look too closely at what was perceived as an affair of honor. My grandfather never told me how he came to be the way he was, or how many others like us there might be."

"I never knew the risks of transformation for some," she added quietly.

Cole was about to speak when Madame Cailletet

grasped his hand and drew him up. "We will barely make it back before dawn. We must hurry," she said.

She no longer held his hand, but let him follow her, retracing their path to her house. Cole had no trouble keeping up with her, but without her touch, was beginning to feel increasingly drained.

Back at the house she led him to a side door and brought him back to the hallway where his room was found. She stood close so that an early riser could not overhear her.

Madame Cailletet took Cole's hand again.

"Be patient, Cole. You will know what I can tell you eventually. After this evening, when we are alone, I am Aurora to you." She shook his hand formally, with a hint of a smile on her lips, and turned back to the stairs, descending to her living quarters.

Cole watched her go, then looked down at the gashed, muddy slippers on his feet and trudged off to his room. As he entered, he was stunned by the orangey dawn light and rushed to close the drapes he had left open. He threw the slippers and robe aside and fell asleep, unclothed, atop the bed.

Cole awoke as he felt a blanket thrown across him. "As a respectable woman, I was most shocked by your backside announcing itself as I came to prepare you for breakfast, Captain," said Bridgett.

Cole rolled over and adjusted the blanket.

"You have dressed my wounds and bathed me. You

have not died of embarrassment before now, but since you are struggling with my lack of pants, I will endeavor to have some when you enjoy my company in the future. Besides, you could have knocked at the door."

"You are a sick man, so I thought you might be unconscious," said Bridgett. "What have you done? Your slippers are destroyed and your feet are dirty and bloody," she said.

"I went for a little stroll."

"I told you men are pigs. Here on the cabinet is a basin of warm water. Wash. There is clothing as well. Sergeant Miller will be here shortly to escort you to the Officer's Breakfast, where he will introduce you."

Cole found the clothing set out for him, a loose shirt and gray trousers. After washing in the tabletop basin, he shaved and dressed before Sergeant Miller arrived for him.

"Now you do look a smashing young gentleman ready for some good sport. You rise from the dead most amazingly. Come along, the remaining young gentlemen await your presence," said Miller.

"Remaining... you mean some have left?" Cole asked.

"Yes, most of the officers have gone. Many of the enlisted, too. There are rumors the war will be over soon. I think they want men back with their units if they are able."

"There have been rumors for months," said Cole.

"Indeed, but there seems more of a smell of an end about recently," said Sergeant Miller.

"Well, I hope your nose is most perspicacious, Sergeant."

At the dining area, which was on the same floor as Cole's room, four men in uniform sat about a small table.

"Gentlemen, I present Dr. Cole Sterling, well on his way to recovery from wounds inflicted by our devious foes," announced Sergeant Miller and excused himself.

William Malvern was a tall, thin English lieutenant. Gary Cooper was average in height but the fit of his American captain's uniform showed off his remarkable, athletic build.

Fred Brindell was a 40ish English captain. He appeared annoyed that his breakfast was delayed for Cole's arrival.

The fourth officer, Sam Lincoln, was a gangly young American lieutenant that Cole doubted shaved more than once a week. He shook Cole's hand heartily before they all retook their seats to be served by another one of Madame Cailletet's many servants.

The four men attacked their plates with relish. Cole was surprised that what appeared to be a tasty breakfast repulsed him. He toyed with some cheese and bread but ate only a few bites. The other men ignored his lack of appetite, no doubt attributing its absence to his injuries.

Captain Brindell said, "We are here in this window-less room because of you, Captain Sterling. We normally dine in a more spacious and sunlit room. We were told you could not withstand sunlight, even through window glass. We find it odd that you now have the same malady as our gracious hostess and therapist."

"Odd is a tame word for the affliction, Captain Brindell," said Cole. "I am a physician and have no satisfactory explanation. Madame Cailletet claims to have given me a transfusion of her blood. How she knew it would not kill me I cannot fathom, nor do I understand the resulting light sensitivity. I speculate there were certain substances in her blood that have produced this effect. My body will probably neutralize these materials eventually," said Cole. "But, please, tell me about your progress here, this place is not what I would expect in a war zone," continued Cole.

William Malvern spoke first, carefully choosing his words. "We are part of an experiment. We all have the diagnosis of neurasthenia; our nervous systems are casualties of war. As you know, when things are thick, no one really cares if we can be coaxed out of a fetal position, we get a short rest and we reenter the fight. The staff officers hope we can hold ourselves together until they are ready to send us home. Then they give us rest, quiet, and tell us not to discuss our experiences. We are to forget the mayhem and hopefully reenter the fight if still needed.

"We English are experienced with this after all these years, but that does not mean we are successful in rehabilitating our men for safe return to war. Such men often expose themselves to reckless risks and are killed or they collapse again into a state dangerous to their comrades. Madame Cailletet is a lay therapist and has excellent training in the damaged mind. She studied with a well-known Swiss doctor. "

"The French and English, and now the Americans ,allow her to use us for her experimental fodder. Mostly enlisted, but a few officers, I suppose, to see if her methods apply equally to different social classes. Under her care, we still get quiet and rest, but we also get to talk with her and among ourselves about the war or other things. Some men cannot speak of what they have seen, but Madame Cailletet believes that just talking with other soldiers and hearing their internal struggles still helps such men."

Captain Brindell interjected, "I am not a supporter of this. I think we are encouraging whining and are undermining discipline. A soldier has to expect to die, to be maimed, to see his mates killed. We kill the enemy and he kills us. Talking and carrying on about it will not change anything, and it melts the steel that has to be in a soldier's spine and weakens his unquestioning response to orders to place himself in the face of danger."

Brindell paused, then said, "You must excuse me. There are soldiers downstairs who need me to write letters for them to send home."

After Brindell exited the room, Gary Cooper said, "Brindell, as you can tell, does not approve of this experiment in coddling, as he termed it, and is angry to be assigned here. Fortunately, he is to leave in a few days and will be back with a front line unit. I also need to go downstairs. This is the time of day we have committed to helping our less literate countrymen reassure their families that they are among the living."

Malvern excused himself as well, leaving behind Sam Lincoln, who seemed pleased to be alone with Cole. "We get along well enough, but Brindell is difficult and everyone is waiting for the war to end. A man cannot help but be anxious. Will he see action again or not? I, for one, can live without seeing another dead soldier, even a German one."

Cole tried to get the conversation back to his original question about Madame Cailletet's work.

"Do you think you have been helped by your stay here?" he asked.

"Yes, I got here three weeks ago, and shook so hard I could not drink hot tea without scalding myself. Of late, we can hear the cannon nearby. In spite of that, I have not fallen apart. Other men have done well, too. We can't talk to the enlisted men now, too much light downstairs. After dark, I will introduce you to a few. The officers are careful not to fraternize, but we check on their progress and needs and occasionally join in the music and games. Considering what everyone has seen and done, they mostly seem pretty sane. I will say they benefit from being here, regardless of Brindell's opinion."

Bridgett came in and removed the last of the breakfast dishes and saw that the two men had fresh hot tea.

Sam was subdued in her presence, but could not disguise that he was watching her. Cole teased him as soon as she was gone. "Not the girl next door, is she? I do not think your mother would approve of her as a war souvenir."

Sam blushed. "I do lust for her. You are right, my mother would not approve, but I do imagine her back home with me."

Cole realized Sam was serious. "She is probably ten years older than you, unschooled, and likely experienced in the world. She is not a suitable lady friend for a young officer."

Sam stammered, "I know but all I do is think about her."

Talk to Madame Cailletet. Maybe the strength of the attraction is part of your neurasthenia."

"Oh, I can't do that, she's a woman and Bridgett is her maid."

"I do not know much about psychology and psychiatry, but I do know that when the mind is not balanced, it can create strong fixations that are difficult to control. Madame Cailletet is no doubt comfortable with the concept and will help you."

Sam rose from the table and sheepishly said, "I need to help with the men, too. Excuse me."

Cole shrugged and walked to an adjoining sitting room outfitted with books and old magazines, located a writing desk with pen and paper, and began to write a letter to his mother, hoping that she had not been informed of his injuries by the War Department. With some luck, he would say something helpful to a least one human being today.

Magazines and missives soon tired Cole and he retired to his room with a dusty tome on Roman architecture. There, he soon dozed off, shooing Bridgett away when she came to serve him lunch in his room. She came back in the evening and harangued him into getting out of bed and putting on the evening clothes she laid out for him

~

Cole managed to dress himself in spite of her efforts to dress him. She escorted him to Madame Cailletet's room, which was set up for two to dine. Cole noticed there were few serving dishes, but once again, a dark crystal decanter set in the center of the table.

Madame Cailletet awaited him and invited him to sit across from her.

"You look fatigued, Cole," Madame Cailletet began.

"I feel exhausted. I felt well this morning and now I only want to sleep," Cole replied.

"You are not eating, of course you are weakening."

"I have no appetite, it all repulses me. I am light-headed now thinking about the fine food in your serving dishes, Madame Cailletet."

"I told you to call me Aurora, Cole. I insist," she said.

"Of course, I am delighted to do so. I apologize for my condition."

"You need nourishment, Cole," said Aurora.

She poured dark red liquid from the decanter into a silver goblet near Cole's right hand. "Please join me," she said as she raised her own goblet to her lips.

Wine was not a pleasant thought for Cole, but he took a sip to avoid offending Aurora. Cole had never tasted wine of this richness. The flavor was indescribable: sweet and tangy with an earthy undertone. Cole drake more and soon emptied the goblet. Aurora poured more for him as she sipped from her goblet.

"This is amazing. A moment ago, I was shivering and clutching the edge of my seat, and now I feel warm and flushed, and eager to talk to you on any subject under the sun. My brain is alive again! What is this marvelous mixture? Is it a stimulant mixed with wine?" Cole noticed Aurora's countenance was sad, not festive as he imagined his to be.

"Cole, do not hate me nor judge me. I transformed you to save you. I do not know why. I had to do it. You know much, but not everything. Beings like us do not sustain ourselves with common food, although we can eat a little occasionally. We survive only through drinking blood, ideally human blood. This decanter contains human blood with a bit of carefully selected wine. To you, it now is the nectar of the gods. There is nothing like it in the whole world."

Cole held the goblet on edge and watched the dark liquid glide along the smooth wall. He sniffed the contents and tasted again.

"Why should I believe you? I am surrounded by a sea of blood in this awful war. It does not smell like this. We have all tasted our own blood at some point and it is nothing like this drink," Cole said.

"You are not what you were. You already know you are superior to what you were. Your tastes have changed, too." Aurora raised her goblet. "This is what blood tastes like to you and to me now."

Cole placed his goblet on the table and pushed it away. "I am not a ghoul. Did this blood come from the dying men?" he asked angrily.

"Some of their blood is here. Their blood was leaking away and their death imminent. You and I benefit from their gift but the blood was removed to make their demise less painful and prolonged," Aurora said.

"They did not give their blood and I am certain that

when alive and well, they would have been horrified by what you have done," said Cole, icily.

Aurora started to reply but only looked away at the logs burning briskly in the fireplace.

"A war is convenient for your thirst but you have lived this way long before the war. How do you get your blood?"

Aurora seemed relieved to answer this question. "I have agents in several larger cities. We pay people for their blood. They are poor and glad to have the money. They are told the blood is used by doctors for experiments and for special regenerative elixirs in Switzerland.

"As long as they get their money and some explanation, they are satisfied. It is difficult to get the blood here without spoilage, but my agents have done well in getting enough here for me to drink. The war has interfered with this endeavor and, in spite of what you expect, I have only removed the blood of the dying once before. We rarely have physically damaged soldiers here and almost never dying ones. I suppose that is one reason I treated you. I, unlike you, am not experienced in watching young men die."

"But you picked me to save," said Cole.

"I told you I do not know why."

"I told the other officers at lunch that I believed the sun sensitivity would wear off, but now it seems that I will live out my life in the shadows and drinking blood like a fiend. Am I a vampire?" asked Cole with disgust.

Aurora smiled. "You are alive, not the undead. You are human and cannot turn into a bat or dog or wisp of vapor and, regrettably, you can't produce fangs. I do not know of a name for our kind or even if there are many others. I have only known of two besides ourselves."

Cole put his elbow on the table and rested his head in his palms, rubbing his forehead with his fingers. "I feel drained emotionally. I don't know how I would feel if I was struck with shrapnel and awoke to a life changing condition, such as the loss of two or three limbs or my sight—an event that forever changed the anticipated remainder of my life. This is similar. I can't be a surgeon or hope to have a family. I am an outcast living in the dark."

"Cole, I have lived and thrived. People need not know about your need for blood, and they will come to grips with your avoiding the sun as a disease. You may not be able to live the life of a surgeon, but you are a doctor and can find ways to see patients if you wish. You can learn from me and others and practice as a psychiatrist. You can see patients in your home under controlled conditions. There are many possibilities.

"I understand your grief at losing your chosen specialty and your dreams for your life, but dreams change in the course of life, regardless of our wishes. We are God or fate's pawns. Railing against this will not help. You trained to serve others and you can do so again more easily than you think."

"Who knows about the two of us?" asked Cole.

"Several of my staff know about the blood but they do not understand everything about my need for it," said Aurora.

She continued, "Please let me help you. Please watch what I do with the men here. If you want to do work like this, I will introduce you to my trainer, Professor Karl Jung. He will counsel you, guide you in ways I cannot."

Cole stood up and said, "Aurora, I understand that you saved my life, although that is nearly impossible for me to comprehend. I should be grateful but my overwhelming thought is that this is a crime against nature, and it would have been better to have died. I do not know that I can live like this, drinking blood. To chastise or offend you is not my wish, but I have to leave now. My outrage is too great."

Cole turned and walked to the door and was pleased that Aurora did not call him back.

For several days after this last revelation by Aurora, Cole walked the forest alone every night. Aurora did not appear.

Cole spent his days reading and observing some of the group talk sessions for the enlisted men. Aurora did not attend as usual, but left Sergeant Miller in charge following her instructions on how to encourage the men in sharing their fears and painful experiences. The men were desultory and bored, and Miller was clearly frustrated in his new assignment.

Brindell and Malvern left to return to rejoin combat units and Gary Cooper said he had orders to leave as soon as someone came for him. Sam was Cole's only comrade, having chosen to ignore the awkward conversation about Bridgett. Cole carefully avoided any reference to her.

In spite of the increasingly cool days, some of the men walked to the stream on the property and indulged in quick dips, usually au naturel. After a vigorous early evening jaunt, Cole decided to brave the water for a few minutes. The other men only bathed in the warmth of the day, so Cole was alone as he stripped off his clothes and plopped into the cool stream. Given his flushed state, the cold water was intense and discouraged him from more than a brief splash about in the gurgling flow.

As he skipped out onto the bank, he heard his name called. At the tree edge, sitting on a blanket in the grass, was Bridgett. Cole was so startled, he momentarily forgot his nudity.

"Come here, Cole. I have an extra blanket for you to dry," Bridgett said.

Cole made a feeble attempt to satisfy his modesty using the proffered blanket and after wrapping himself, sat next to Bridgett.

"Why are you here, Bridgett?" he asked.

"I know you walk by here every evening. I thought I would wait for you. You were like a little boy playing in the water."

"You could have called to me."

"I enjoyed your exhibition. Why would I spoil it?" she said.

Bridgett pulled Cole on top of her and began to kiss him as she ran her hands down his back to his buttocks.

Cole pulled her blouse up and caressed her breasts

with his hands as he explored her nipples with his tongue.

Bridgett pulled her dress up to her waist and took Cole inside her. The thick grass cushioned their vigorous lovemaking and Cole soon spent himself and lay gasping for breath next to Bridgett.

She laughed and pushed him onto his stomach, straddled him, and began to massage his back with her luxurious bare breasts. Cole lay in a warm cocoon of bliss with the undulating Bridgett above him and the soft cushioned blanket beneath him. Eventually, Bridgett rolled him over and mounted him for another bout of lovemaking, this time slower, prolonged, and ending with Bridgett moaning and digging her nails into his upper back and shoulders.

This time she fell off him and lay panting by his side.

Once she had caught her breath, she grasped Cole's face between her hands.

"Cole, I know the world has no place for us together. You live in your station. I, in mine. But we were meant to be together tonight and never regret that," said Bridgett.

She rose, adjusted her hair and clothes, and thrust the blankets into a small sack.

"I have to hurry back before there are too many questions." She kissed him one last time and ran into the woods toward the house.

Cole stood forlornly, watching her running away without looking back. He dressed and took a roundabout path back to avoid appearing too close to Bridgett's arrival. He could still smell on himself the scent of

Bridgett's perfume and powder He felt a little sad that, in a way, he had betrayed Sam with Bridgett, but he was too satisfied with his sexual encounter to mourn Sam's theoretical betrayal. The matter of fact acceptance by Bridgett of her and Cole's separate destinies was more disturbing to Cole. The logic was fact inescapable but in the pit of Cole's stomach there was sadness and longing.

Fortunately, by the time he reached the house, he could hear the men singing an ancient Welsh mining song and joined them around the piano, even taking a glass of beer from Sergeant Miller as he tried to decipher the meaning of the raucous lyrics.

The next morning, Colette brought several books and a journal to Cole along with a carafe of blood.

"Where is Bridgett, Colette? She usually brings what I need in the morning."

"Bridgett is occupied with her business and her business does not involve you," said Colette coldly.

To hide his annoyance, Cole asked about the books.

"Madame wants you to read them. She said you need to move on with your new life."

Satisfied that she had put Cole in his place, Colette left the room.

The books all dealt with psychoanalysis but the truly interesting item was the journal with Aurora's notes during her apprenticeship with Dr. Karl Jung, training as a lay analyst. The notes covered Jung's comments about an assortment of conditions and individual cases, but the real gold was at the end. Aurora summarized an approach to the patient, which Cole suspected was a powerful guide to efficiently identifying a patient's core problem.

Cole spent the day absorbing the material as best he could. He often referred to other materials to better elucidate the concepts in her journal. He was surprised at how the approach described by Aurora could be applied to so many different situations.

Just as Cole sensed the sunset through the heavy curtains and experienced the usual restlessness this elicited, Colette came to him and formally invited him to dine with Madame.

Cole was still angry and considered declining but realized the childishness of this impulse and accepted solemnly.

An hour later he sat in Aurora's room face to face at a small table with only a ruby-colored decanter of blood and wine between them.

Cole spoke with her about his day and asked her a few questions, but Aurora answered him perfunctorily. Cole was distracted himself. He had to admit he had never seen a more beautiful woman. Aurora's long hair, radiant in the light from the fire, hung loosely about the shoulders and the open collar of the oriental dressing gown she wore. The gown was vibrant in color and seemed the perfect accompaniment to her skin and hair.

Cole saw a hint of gossamer lace beneath the gown.

He was flustered by a heady melange of anger with Aurora for upsetting his life, her apparent denial to him of access to Bridgett, and now her disinterested attitude regarding the very subject she had encouraged him to study. Anger and lust were forming a powerful vortex of emotion in Cole, which thankfully was swept away by Aurora saying softly, "I have invited Father Grevy to dinner tomorrow night and would like you to join us. I have known him my entire life. I think it is important that you meet him."

"Why?" asked Cole simply.

"We live in a different world from others, but we are still God's creatures. Our sanity and our souls depend on our never forgetting this. Father Grevy is often irreverent but he does help when I most need his assistance. You can start a new life. I don't know if he can inspire you in any way now, but the time may come when he can. Besides, I think you will like Father Grevy; he is good company."

"Then I look forward to dining with the two of you," said Cole.

Aurora lapsed into silence and seemed sad to Cole. He tried again to direct her attention back to the intellectual. "Your journal is fascinating. You should publish it. Your summary of an approach to treatment is outstanding," said Cole.

"I doubt Jung would sanction such a publication and the summary is my interpretation of his method. I have probably distorted much of what he thinks," said Aurora. "He is rather eclectic in the design of treatment plans. In many ways, it is a snapshot of his views several years ago when I spent time with him. I married shortly afterwards and for a while I did not pursue my studies or work with patients."

"You do not talk of your husband. Is he away at war?" asked Cole.

"I do not know. Our marriage was ended before the war." Aurora's gaze had shifted to her hands in her lap. After a while, she continued.

"We married in our thirties and after years of inability to conceive, I finally became pregnant but miscarried after a few weeks. We were both devastated, but my husband became erratic and belligerent. We lived in Paris and even my husband's prominent family could not prevent his increasingly boorish excesses. He insulted a young man's new wife and it became an affair of honor. Both men belonged to the same fencing club and they retreated to private grounds to settle this in the old way.

"I am told they fought for nearly half an hour with much damage to each other. Finally, the young man plunged his foil into my husband, then staggered backward and dropped to the ground dead. My husband's family rushed him to our home. They had a doctor waiting there but he could do nothing and advised me to summon a priest. I sent everyone away and did for my husband what I did for you and he recovered as you did."

Tears slowly poured down Aurora's cheeks, but she brushed them away and hushed Cole's attempts to comfort her.

"Marie-Henri, that is his name, no longer resembled the man I married. He brutalized me and turned to every debauchery in Paris. He welcomed his confinement to the dark of night and savored the taking of blood. He found a thousand disgusting ways to extract what he wanted without care for anyone. His family could not suppress his crimes, but they managed to get him out of Paris before the police took him.

"My family took what evidence of Marie-Henri's debauchery they could collect and was able to get the church to annul my marriage. I returned home and began to try to help those with mental problems and the poor, in general, to compensate for my sin in making a troubled man into a monster."

Aurora continued to cry and Cole did not try to stop her. He merely placed a hand on top of hers and asked, "But aren't you being too hard on yourself? You said he changed after the miscarriage. He was an unstable personality who could not cope with that. You tried to save his life. You could not know that his mental deterioration was so severe that his fragile psyche would shatter with his transformation."

Aurora cried harder. "He told me he had wanted to die, that I had prolonged a life of unendurable pain. I had trained to help those who suffer mentally, those with broken hearts, but the one person who I wanted to help the most I could not help at all. Instead, I made him into a man with no love of God or man left in his soul," said Aurora. "I have been sick with worry, Cole, that you could also become a sociopath or worse after your transformation."

"I have many faults, mostly petty I suppose, but I do not think I am all that different from what I was. Except I am very angry with fate and with you." Cole could not resist glaring at Aurora. "But I do not want to hurt you or anyone else, with the exception of the bastard who shot me when I was down and helpless. I drink the blood you provide with a pinch of bitterness and disgust. I cannot imagine taking it from someone by force."

Cole sat back in his chair and said softly, "I cannot absolve you of guilt for transforming me, but you did not make me a monster. Your conscience should be clear of that."

Aurora's eyes were red and swollen but she had managed to stop crying. She wiped her cheeks with her handkerchief and poured him more of the blood wine mixture. Tonight the wine seemed headier , with Cole feeling flushed from the heat of the fire, the drink, and their raw emotions.

Aurora unbuttoned the top button of her gown and after adjusting the fire screen to deflect some of the heat away from them, stood in front of Cole and said simply, "I am sorry I have hurt you. Please try to forgive me."

Cole took her hand in his and said, "I will try."

He kissed her hand after gazing at her longingly, then pulled her into his lap. He began to kiss her lips and caress her neck. Aurora melted into his arms with a soft sigh ,humming a tune barely perceptible. She gently rocked as he removed her gown.

Beneath the gown, Aurora wore a thin delicate lace camisole, which Cole removed as he slowly traced her body, from her knees to her shoulders, in soft caresses with his hands. He carried Aurora to her canopy bed and lay with her in a feverish embrace that seemed outside time as they made love until nearly dawn.

Aurora sent Cole back to his room. As he looked back at her from her door, she said, "Captain, do you see the ornate box on my side table?" Aurora gestured from her bed , and sat upright against several pillows. Cole was so entranced by her nude form that he struggled to view the object she singled out.

"Yes, I see it," he whispered.

"My great grandfather brought it from the Orient many years ago. I keep only my most precious objects there. You could not know but Bridgett is not just my maid. I attended her birth and helped to rear her when her mother, my favorite maid, died. I thought you should know these things to better understand my warning, my beloved Captain, to you that if you touch her again, I will be most happy to place your testicles in my special box."

Cole restrained a smile and, bowing slightly, withdrew saying, "I will be honored to respect your wishes, Madame Cailletet."

Cole was pleased that in the following days, he was with Aurora daily, working with the remaining men in groups and individually.

Aurora used a range of techniques, dream interpretation, word association, and even hypnosis to push forward in improving the mental health of her charges. She frequently coaxed from the men their horrific accounts of the most awful parts of the war.

This part was difficult for Cole. He had seen the carnage they described up close. He had been insulated by the need to repair the physical damage and intentionally did not want to dwell on the terror and pain that preceded the arrival of the torn flesh that moved in a bloody parade across his surgical table. Now he had to absorb the horror a second time as he connected the soldiers anguish and terror in the field with the mangled bodies that he had often futilely tried to repair.

Cole's only respite from this excursion into the labyrinth of the war damaged psyche were early evening walks with Sam. They strolled on the cultivated grounds of the estate and talked of their lives back home. Cole mostly listened to Sam as he described his near idyllic childhood in Missouri.

There were endless tales of juvenile pranks, boyhood crushes, and Sam's reprobate relatives. Sam longed to return to his family a swaggering young hero. Sam's descriptions were so vivid that Cole could picture the warm community Sam had left. Cole had never had a close family and Sam's loving descriptions helped Cole to escape the pain that nagged at him relentlessly.

Bridgett eventually returned and acted as if their encounter had never happened. She was her usual bright self, never mentioning her absence or their new connection.

When Cole tried to question her, she merely smiled and touched her finger to his lips.

One morning she brought the usual items for Cole, leaned over, and whispered, "I told you we could never be together," and nipped his earlobe.

She laughed and walked away before Cole could respond.

Cole stared at the books before him, treatises on

psychology and psychiatry. He shook his head. "If I understood all this, I still could never understand women."

Somehow Cole was comforted by Bridgett's proximity and that she seemed content to return to her usual life. His life was too disordered now to want to ruminate on the odd situation with Bridgett and its long-term implications. Dinner with Father Grevy was another respite from the horrors of war. Cole could smell Father Grevy's pipe as he approached the drawing room where dinner was to be served for the three of them. Father Grevy had already secured a larger brandy before Cole's arrival. Short, rotund, and ruddy, Father Grevy managed a commanding presence in his cassock with his ample gesticulations and booming voice.

He appraised Cole as if he were a prize pig up for auction. Cole was surprised that Aurora did not complain of the pungent smoke that was already clouding the room.

After greeting Father Grevy and Aurora, Cole sat in an armchair snuggled between theirs.

"Aurora tells me you are like many who have come to this war; you will not return as you were. At least you are not one of the unfortunates for whom I have administered last rites. I suppose there is solace in that," said the priest.

Cole looked at Aurora.

"Yes, he knows," Aurora said softly. "He is my oldest living friend and confessor."

Cole inwardly cringed at the thought of Aurora

discussing their relationship with this crude, sweaty little man.

"I would have thought that as a priest you would have considered us pariahs, doomed outcasts unfit to be within the walls of a church," said Cole with more edge to his voice than he intended.

"Direct and to the point. An American trait, I hear. Yes, the church does not condone the drinking of blood, but the Old Testament prohibition is related to permitting animal meat and avoiding animal blood, not humans. Your peculiar condition is not addressed. Since you have a right to sustain yourself, I doubt you violate church rules if you act within the overall framework of the faith."

Father Grevy paused to pull on his pipe and blow a sphere of smoke out into the center of the room. "But of course my view is mine. I have not consulted with my superiors."

And you will not contact them about any of this because Aurora is your friend, thought Cole. Cole knew his Old Testament well enough to know that blood is described consistently as forbidden. Particularly the verse in Leviticus, "Ye shall eat the blood of no manner of flesh." It's absolutely clear. Cole also suspected that Aurora had been less than candid about the source of all the blood they drink.

Aurora's face was ashen. Cole did not want to hurt her more than he already had.

"Father Grevy, I apologize. I am struggling with my new condition. I judge myself. It is difficult to not view others as judging me."

Father Grevy interjected, "No need to apologize, my son. A man is to be commended for viewing his life within a moral framework. We are rational beings. A man is supposed to evaluate himself and weigh his actions as he thinks they would be viewed by God. Here, add a little brandy to that hideous concoction that Aurora has poured for you."

Cole poured the proffered spirit into his goblet, delighted to see Aurora's eyes shining with the change in atmosphere within the room.

"So, tell me, my son, are you committed to switching from surgery to psychiatry? Aurora seems to think you have no choice, but an intelligent man always has choices. I suspect she has ulterior motives in advocating that position, since it keeps you near."

"Father, that is rude. I never said Cole had no other option than psychiatry and he is free to make his own decisions. Brandy makes your tongue wag too freely," said Aurora.

Father Grevy laughed. "See, Cole, see how she treats me. I am sure no other in my congregation would say my tongue wags too much." Father Grevy laughed even harder at this obvious untruth. Cole smiled, warming to this jovial man who could laugh at himself so heartily.

"I was not impressed by psychiatry in medical school, but now that I have had the opportunity to read within the field, I am fascinated. I see, here at Aurora's house, these fine young men, wounded in body, mind, and spirit. Medicine and surgery are limited in healing their flesh but nearly hopeless in restoring their psyches. Beyond the immediate issue of neurasthenia, I now recognize that many men came to this war damaged, limited in their ability to love and engage with others.

"I have to understand these problems also if I am to help these men recover from the mental damage they encountered in combat. There is no comprehensive guide to helping them. This is a challenge that appeals to me and I am learning from Aurora and my reading with every new day. I do not know where I am going at present. To protect my sanity, I am taking each day as it comes."

"A wise decision. Today is God's gift to us; tomorrow is uncertain and music makes today better," Father Grevy barked with emphasis, slapping his thigh and lumbering up from the cushiony depths of his armchair. He waddled over to the spinet in one corner of the drawing room and began to pound out a humorous and slightly ribald tune he had learned at seminary. Father Grevy's singing was surprisingly good, especially considering the bare adequacy of his piano playing.

Cole and Aurora stood around the piano as he ran through his repertoire of folk songs, popular songs from his young, and even Stephen Foster selections. Father Grevy's delivery was similar with all of his choices. He worked hard at his art and his face was florid with perspiration dripping from his brow as he finally concluded his recital.

Cole and Aurora applauded him and helped him back to his chair where he returned to downing swigs of brandy.

He turned the conversation to the local citizenry. Cole found Aurora and the good Father's gossiping about his parishioners enlightening and time passed pleasantly until Father Grevy had regained his strength and declared he was ready for bed.

Aurora summoned one of her servants to take him home and Cole wished him a good night, delighted for Aurora and his sake that he now had a comfortable relationship with someone so important to her.

After one of the servants readied the room, Aurora locked the door and had Cole drape a bear rug in front of the fireplace. After Aurora had Cole recline on the rug, she dropped her gown on the floor and began to methodically strip Cole as he lay on his back. She refused to let him touch her as she did this, gliding her hands over his body and softly kissing him until she had him completely naked as the fire crackled before them.

They made love twice, perspiring in the warmth of the flicking flames before the hearth. By the time they finished, the fire had died down and Cole covered their now chilly bodies with a soft blanket as they drifted off to sleep with Aurora resting on Cole's chest.

A few days after Father Grevy's visit, Cole relaxed in his room experiencing his usual excitement as twilight coursed into the night. He intended to walk with Sam on the grounds in the freshness of the new evening before supper was served.

Muffled shouting, followed by women screaming, broke his reverie. He was already standing as he now heard rifle fire near the house. He ran from his room and out into the night with an American revolver that Sam had somehow acquired and insisted that Cole keep hidden in his room.

Only a trace of twilight remained as Cole rushed out of the house. Fortunately his enhanced vision quickly allowed him to see several German soldiers pulling two women into one of the outbuildings used by the cooks. A man's body lay nearby.

As he closed the distance to the structure, Cole saw Sam run into the building firing a small pistol. Even with his heightened senses, Cole struggled to take in the gruesome display within the small room as he bounded through the door.

Colette lay on her back with her skirt pushed up to her neck. A dead soldier lay between her legs and face down on her chest. She was screaming with fear in a screeching sound Cole had never heard from a human before.

Bridgett lay on her back with two dead soldiers on her. One between her legs, and the other sitting on her arms and face. The man on her head had fallen back against the wall, still resting on her face. A fourth soldier lay wounded at Bridgett's feet.

Bridgett had fought ferociously and did not intend to suffocate in the usual way as she was raped. To terminate her struggle, the waiting solder had smashed her throat with the butt of his rifle. Sam had shot all four men and now lay at Bridgett's side where he had fallen after the soldier with the rifle had been able to get off a round at the berserk Sam.

Cole forced himself away from the dead Sam and

Bridgett and removed the corpse from Colette. As he tried to comfort Colette, he heard a pistol shot reverberate in the room as Sergeant Miller dispatched the wounded man, screaming, "You bloody Huns, the war will be over in days! What have you done? What have you done?"

The old man began to sob and was led away by several of his young charges. Cole had two of the Sergeant's remaining men escort Colette to the house while he sent others for a small cart to bring Sam's body back to the house. He pushed the dead men off Bridgett and, after arranging her clothing, he carried her to Aurora in his arms.

They buried Bridgett in a fine drizzle at twilight. The gloom of the extinguishing day complemented the moroseness of their hearts. Father Grevy had spoken in church lovingly of Bridgett and the good she had done in her short life. His service at graveside was traditional and brief. While fewer were at the grave than in church, the assembly was large, with townspeople, Aurora's patients and household gathered in shocked grief at Bridgett's loss.

So many had died in recent years, including civilians, but with the war's end so near and their sector quiet, Bridgett's loss seemed especially senseless and a test of their faith.

Cole suspected the depth of their grief was in part a sorrowing for themselves at having to endure another pointless death in this never-ending war. Cole was touched that Aurora had buried Bridgett at the edge of her family burial area and not in the adjoining long-term family servants' plot. Bridgett's final resting place would be near Aurora's.

Aurora received visitors for several days after the funeral from a number of socially prominent people who had not been at the services. This was very difficult for her; many of these well- meaning callers did not know that Bridgett was not just a favorite maid, and made awkward condolences, some even discussing in a mundane way possible suitable replacements for the lost servant.

While more sensitive souls redirected their conversation, seeing Aurora's distress at this topic, others persisted until Aurora burst into tears and excused herself.

Cole made himself available to Aurora but did not intrude on her when she needed to be alone. On the third day after the funeral, Aurora insisted on meeting again with her patients and worked with Cole on his reading. She concentrated on mundane topics and avoided abstract expansive topics. Cole assumed she wanted to focus her mind on the work but was afraid to allow herself a free ranging perspective that might draw her into too close a look at her own thoughts and feelings at this vulnerable time.

Less than a week after the funeral, the household learned that the day of the Armistice would be the 11th hour of the 11th day of November. Their joy at hearing this was tempered by Bridgett's pointless death, and the thought of the inevitable carnage that would continue without an immediate Armistice. In any event, Sergeant Miller prepared all the men to leave Aurora's beneficent care.

The estate experienced a flurry of activity after the Armistice. Aurora began the process of reclaiming her home from the barracks it had become on the lower floors. Workers were everywhere restoring, cleaning, and painting. Old art works and tapestries were reestablished in their former domains and Cole saw the staff's faces brighten as they saw what seemed like old friends who had survived the war back in their familiar places.

November was not Spring, but at least for a while, Spring had come to their lives again.

Aurora informed the mayors of nearby towns that they should send troubled men returning from deployment to her to benefit from the therapy she had developed over the course of the war. She was clear that the men's lodging was no longer her concern. Her home was restored to previous use.

After Aurora had dealt with the most pressings issues of moving from war to peace, she wrote Karl Jung requesting that Cole and she be allowed to visit him in Switzerland. She wanted Jung's blessing for her tutoring Cole in the art of psychoanalysis. Jung responded with alacrity.

Aurora showed Cole Jung's letter of reply. He warmly welcomed communication from one of his most delightful, memorable students, and looked forward to meeting her student and close friend. With her letter, Aurora had delicately allowed Jung to surmise that she and Cole were much more than student-mentor and friend. Aurora wanted Jung's blessing mostly because of their relationship.

As Cole pursued his career, he might require a letter from Jung acknowledging his having met Cole and vouchsafing Cole's pedigree of instruction in Jung's methods. Aurora did not want Jung to be unaware of the totality of Aurora's and Cole's relationship.

Cole doubted he would be seeking an academic position in psychiatry where Jung's reference would be critical, but he understood Aurora's caution and appreciated her determination in securing a sound foundation for his future.

In mid December, Cole and Aurora began their long tedious journey by rail to Zurich. The train service was erratic and trying. Aurora had arranged first class for them, but there were no sleeping arrangements and even first class compartments were cold and crowded. Many of their fellow travelers were French businessmen looking for markets in Switzerland and assistance with financing, which was currently nearly unobtainable in France. They wore expensive suits that had seen better days and they prattled on to the beautiful mysterious young woman who shared their compartment about their factories and their wondrous prospects now that the Hun had been beaten back.

Cole imagined that they wanted to impress the beautiful lady but also suspected that they discerned that Aurora was wealthy and perhaps might show an interest in sponsoring their grandiose business schemes. Cole was of little interest to them, a tiresome leftover American from the war, who in their unstated estimation would be better off back on the other side of the Atlantic.

Aurora was, as usual, a social gem, kind and gentle. Cole could tell she was tired and wished to quietly enjoy their travel together, but she had been bred to always be on stage as a landed aristocrat and lady of the manor. She would struggle to keep her persona in place regardless of her fatigue.

To the consternation of all, at another one of the too frequent station stops, a tall, severe looking , late middle-aged man entered their compartment. He scarcely managed to find enough room to accommodate his well-muscled frame. He sat across from Aurora and Cole, and after group introductions, watched Aurora silently as she continued to banter with her audience.

In spite of the poor heating, their compartment had become by now stuffy and claustrophobic. A suggestion to have supper in the dining car was quietly embraced by all of the group except Cole, Aurora, and the new arrival. Cole and Aurora would wait and have a glass of wine after the dinner rush.

Once the three of them were alone, the other man spoke. "I apologize for staring at you, Madame Cailletet, but I met you some time ago. I did not use my old title when I introduced myself, but I am former Paris police inspector, Jacques Moreau."

Aurora visibly started and her eyes widened in surprise. "But of course, Inspector Moreau, I should have known you instantly. You were so kind to me in those trying times. I apologize profusely, but I must confess that I have used great mental effort to avoid recollections of all that humiliation and sorrow, and your appearance is unexpected and out of context." Aurora flushed with embarrassment, stammering her excuse.

Inspector Moreau smiled kindly, "Unlike you, I have aged poorly since we last met more than five years ago. I wouldn't expect to be readily recognizable, but you truly seem untouched by time. A man could not forget such a beautiful and engaging lady."

Aurora blushed some more. "You are as charming as I recall, Inspector." Aurora leaned toward him. "Please tell me what you are doing on this train. You say you are retired. Are you on holiday?"

"I am retired from the Paris Police, but I do consulting work for the French Government regarding international crime. I assisted with the failed effort to establish an international criminal police congress in Monaco in 1914. After the war, the government continued to use my expertise to help with the coordination of efforts to defeat crime operating across borders. And all of that is a prelude to the things I would like to relate to you. You understandably wish to forget the scandal attached to your former husband but for your protection, you need to be appraised of certain more recent details.

"Before the war, your former husband and his companions repeatedly escaped serious criminal charges for their, let's just say, actions against several young women. They apparently used bribery, intimidation, and legal shenanigans to extricate themselves from convictions for anything other than minor offenses.

"With the outbreak of the war, we set out to arrest the German Baron Gerbold, who had become your husband's most notorious companion and who may have been most responsible for his ignoble behavior. But, we learned that Gerbold had left France just before the hostilities commenced and had taken your husband with him, we suspect, to Berlin. We went back and looked at our files and realized that many incidents listed young and middle-aged French military officers in proximity. None were linked to the criminal acts, but we began to realize that Gerbold was making a point of attracting lusty older officers and naive young officers into compromising positions.

"We could not pursue our suspicions easily, most of the men were away on duty. Fortunately, military officers gossip at least almost as much as their civilian counterparts. Eventually, we had confirmation that after some of Gerbold's retreats, some men implied to their friends that Gerbold had finagled them into potentially career destroying situations. We were eventually able to talk directly to two individuals. The senior officer denied any impropriety and angrily threatened us with reprisal if we continued to besmirch his good name. The young lieutenant was a different proposition. We interviewed him after a brief tour at the front and he collapsed into a wailing, crying, desolate shell of his former self.

"The whole time he was away engaged with the enemy, as he watched his men and fellow officers die horribly in the mud, his conscience gnawed at him. He had been forced to give Gerbold information about expected deployments and unit readiness in the event of war.

"At the time, he did not want to face disgrace before his family and the end of his military career if his sodomitical acts were revealed. He thought the information he provided was of little merit and real prospects of war unlikely. Now he had returned home early for shell shock, but his real incapacitating affliction was his unrelenting guilt at the thought that even one man would not return home to his loved ones because of his cowardice in dealing with Gerbold."

No doubt Gerbold had coerced similar officers into divulging privileged information to him. "You think Marie-Henri was a party to this odious entrapment, for the purpose of espionage?" interjected Aurora. "His family is prominent in French military history. I would have thought he would have died before collaborating with Gerbold in this."

Her face was flushed and her eyes flashed. Cole thought she still puts limits to the expansiveness of Cartan's bad behavior. She reluctantly accepted that a man she respected and adored could become a criminal manipulator of young women, but she could not fathom him as a traitor to his once beloved country. Inspector

Moreau was embarrassed by Aurora's fiery indignation. He weighed his words carefully.

"Based on their extensive travel together and from all accounts we know to date, it seems impossible to envision that your ex-husband did not know of Gerbold's intentions. As to whether he was an active or passive participant, I cannot speculate. All accounts mention Cartan's extensive drug usage. Perhaps Gerbold intentionally fogged Cartan's intellect, but given that there are multiple incidents, over a period of time, this would stretch credibility beyond reasonable boundaries."

Aurora had sunk back in her seat, her face struggling to register the complex mixture of emotions she was experiencing. The Inspector said softly, "I did not tell you these things out of cruelty since they involved an individual you have already renounced. I tell you because Gerbold and Cartan are once again creating incidents.

"They have been seen recently in two French speaking areas, Geneva in Switzerland and Luxembourg, to be specific. Admittedly, their destinations may not have been related to the use of French in these locations, but it is interesting and we have asked police in French speaking areas of Europe to notify us of their presence."

"They are an odious and dangerous pair, and I believe you need to be aware of their activities should you encounter them." Moreau reached in his waistcoat producing at length a business card, which he handed to Aurora. He then stood and bowed slightly.

"I apologize for causing you pain but, he sighed heavily before he continued, I could not in good conscience not inform you of a possible source of embarrassment or of threat to your person. I will now take my dinner."

~

After Moreau left the compartment, Cole grasped Aurora's hand. "Are you all right," he asked.

Aurora smiled wearily and tears ran down her cheeks. "I have great guilt for my part in making Marie-Henri what he is today. After all these years, I have finally accepted my guilt and because I heard nothing of him, I had come to peace with his memory. Now, I find that his criminality continued on unabated while I dreamily went about my daily life. I cannot be all right knowing that a monster I helped create still roams the land."

By now Aurora was crying such that she could not continue speaking.

"Aurora, you know that the transformation does not make a person evil. You and I have the same morality we had before we changed. I know you believe Marie-Henri was a good man before his transformation, but he may have hid his unsavory deeds from you and mislead you about the purity of his heart. Ultimately, this is all on him. The transformation revealed and unleashed a narcissistic and psychopathic personality, nothing more. You, with complete purity of motive, attempted to help him. You cannot take responsibility for his choices," comforted Cole.

"There is no peace for me knowing how much damage Marie-Henri continues to inflict. Noble intentions do not make up for liberating the spark that burns down an old forest. I cannot rationalize away my part in starting this reign of horror. I wanted this trip so badly. The war was so awful and the men and their families suffered so horribly. Throughout, I maintained an outward semblance of competence and confidence.

"As Jung would say, my persona was of cool, stony detachment as I saw to the needs of all the people under by roof. This trip with you was to serve as an official end to the madness. I would see my old mentor, let him see how proud I am of you and enjoy our stay in Zurich. Then we would return home and create new lives for ourselves. That is how I saw this journey, a symbolic cleansing and rejuvenation.

"And then Inspector Moreau brought me back to reality, to the ongoing anxiety, uncertainty, and suffering surrounding me. I guess someone like me cannot hope to have a peaceful quiet life." Aurora had stopped crying, but her face was pale and had lost the warmth and vibrancy she had projected an hour ago.

"I will not give you false comfort. I understand your guilty feelings but, rationally, you had no reason to expect a malevolent outcome from your act of love.

"At this point, you have to let Moreau and the police find Marie-Henri and Gerbold, and we will have to be sure that the estate is properly secured against intrusion. Look, we will still have a good trip. We will still enjoy Zurich and see Jung. We will put all this aside for now and concentrate on our needs. And my need right now is for some of that liquid you have chilled in the basket by your feet," said Cole with a smile as he kissed Aurora's cheek.

Aurora smiled, "Of course, a man's hunger will dispel any annoying concerns about dangerous villains lurking in the night." As she rose she said, "Come along, my lovely, I have a sumptuous mixture of a fine blood line and an excellent Bordeaux. We can drink it in the club car. I believe our new friends are in the dining car so we may have some isolation in enjoying our supper."

In Zurich, Cole and Aurora left the train fully covered against the sun, but fortunately, the biting chill of the breezy morning made them seem merely eccentric travelers unfamiliar and unacclimated to cold Swiss winter although they did receive a few curious looks from the peculiar combination of sunglasses and scarf wrapped faces.

Fortunately, they did not have to endure protracted ogling at the station. The hotel had provided a car and chauffeur who handily loaded their luggage and had them on their way to a small, expensive hotel her family had patronized since before Aurora was born.

Aurora was nearly back to her previous good spirits as she related her adventures as a child in the hotel. She had engaged her favorite room and delighted in showing Cole all the nooks and crannies of the hotel she had explored as a child. She asked after bellboys, desk clerks, assistant managers, elevator operators, waiters, and maids of years ago. The current staff puzzled over her questions since so many of these former workers were nearly forgotten names long departed from the hotel and, in most cases, from this earth.

One ancient bellboy remembered Aurora as a child, fussed over her and reminisced with her about cranky desk clerks and ,giggling with her like school children, about a corpulent, flatulent elevator man. Cole enjoyed seeing Aurora in this way. She was a loving companion at home, but he seldom saw this girlish, frothy lightness, and enjoyment of the moment.

After lunch in the hotel, Aurora guided Cole to the Lander Museum, where she homed in on exhibits she enjoyed as a child, particularly medieval armor and weapons. After a few stops at small shops between the museum and the hotel, they returned to their adjacent rooms to ready themselves for a performance of Der Rosenkavalier guest conducted by Richard Strauss at the Stadttheater.

Aurora was ebullient the next morning, happy with euphoric recall of their evening out and with anticipation of their scheduled dinner with her beloved Jung. She dragged Cole about Zurich, happily frittering away their time in obscure shops and book stores.

They finally located the small restaurant favored by Jung in the Altstadt and gratefully settled into a wooden booth with glasses of wine awaiting his arrival. They did not have to wait long before a tall, mustached, sturdy man approached their booth. Aurora glowed as she introduced Cole and Jung.

Jung asked for beer while Aurora quizzed Jung about his family and mutual friends she knew were in close contact with Jung. After a while, Jung turned the conversation to Cole's reading and his experiences with patients at Aurora's estate. Aurora's letters made Cole's previous life and qualifications known to him.

"Are you finding it difficult to make the transition from surgery to a doctor of the mind?" Jung asked.

"I initially felt trapped, doomed by my transition. I could not imagine not identifying diseased or damaged anatomy and resecting and repairing it, possibly saving a life in the process. Philosophically, surgery is such a satisfying, logical process that I struggled against losing that, technically challenging, but straightforward way of serving humanity." Cole laughed, "I must admit I also miss my scalpel and the feel of cutting. I spent years learning to do that with confidence. In many ways, it is part of my being."

"We have many losses in life. We must change, adapt. Those who do it best find new passions. Could you work skillfully on a beating human heart?"

"Certainly not," answered Cole.

"Well, your vocation is to work on the living, pulsating human heart with all its mystery, complexity, sadness, and potential for savagery. That takes knowledge, compassion, intuition, and imagination. From Aurora's letters, I know you are part of the way there. Be patient with yourself, there will be days when you exalt your new skills and, sadly days of great disappointment. Read and listen to good teachers. Fortunately, you have one at your side." Jung smiled and patted Aurora's hand. "Come let's order. I am famished."

Jung enjoyed a hardy meal while Cole and Aurora ate small amounts of cabbage soup largely to preserve the convention of a shared meal.

Jung and Aurora continued to reminisce and occasionally gossip about former colleagues. Jung had indicated he had to return home early and for Aurora their time together was much too short. As they prepared to leave, Aurora excused herself for the ladies' room and Cole used the opportunity to ask a question that had intrigued him for some time.

"Professor, I find it interesting that your accepted Aurora's explanation when she told you of her condition. Most medical men would not have believed her and dismissed her as a student."

"My family has a long history with the paranormal, and I myself have witnessed many things as a child or young man which have no ready explanation. I have written about many seemly nonscientific subjects. I have had to be very cautious about how I discussed these things and the conclusions I reached. As a serious scientist, I cannot expose myself to ridicule, but I am certainly open-minded and do not think that the science and medicine of today explains everything we encounter.

"Aurora showed me enough early on for me to tentatively accept her story and to conclude that she was not delusional. With the passage of time, I became less and less skeptical. Actually, meeting you adds to the weight of evidence in her favor. She claimed to have converted her ex-husband, but I never knew him. Now, I am acquainted with you, yourself a physician. The fact that her malady is transferable certainly suggests a scientific explanation even if I don't understand the mechanistic details.

"On the other hand, I do not understand how or why you subsist on blood, and why you cannot tolerate the sun or why you have enhanced senses and strength.

Those facts have a paranormal character that even for an open mind are difficult to fathom."

With Aurora's return, they left the gemutlichkeit of the little restaurant and braced themselves for the frigid breeze and blowing snow of the Zurich night. As Jung turned his coat collar up around his neck and pulled his gloves on, he watched two policemen take charge of two gaunt men with threadbare coats.

"Likely, former German soldiers with no work at home stealing across the border hoping for work or at least charity. The police are not too harsh here. The men will get fed and will not freeze tonight. I had a premonition of the horror and suffering to come before the war. I do not have a similar premonition of a future war, but I can tell you as a rational man that the anger, pain, and sense of betrayal unleashed by this recent war will certainly soon lead to another, probably more violent war."

The now somber Jung shook their hands, kissed Aurora's cheek, and walked away into a swirl of snow that gave his departure a phantasmagorical character.

Back home at Aurora's estate, Cole and Aurora quickly returned to their familiar routine of seeing patients, expanding their studies, and caring for the property.

Jung had encouraged them to spend time at a mental institution to better understand the full range of abnormal mental processes. Such an institution was located about fifty kilometers away and they began to commute there on a weekly basis for several months. The psychiatrist in charge of the facility looked forward to their weekly visits and gave them good access to his most interesting patients.

Cole came to understand that they were a welcome diversion for the director, and his quid pro quo for allowing their visits was spending an hour of socializing in his office with Cole, having a snifter of brandy to justify the director having a snifter with his guest.

~

In the fall of 1919, Aurora announced that she wanted to go to the 1920 Olympics in Antwerp.

"Are you competing in fencing or gymnastics?"

"Face slapping is actually my sport. I am going for the gold since I contend with habitual insolence," replied Aurora.

"Ah, your tone might suggest that I merely ask when we are to leave."

"See, you are a wise doctor, but you need not pack right away. I want to be at the opening ceremony in August."

"Aren't the games spread from April to September? I am glad you do not plan to be there for every event."

"We will see the opening ceremony and those events around that time. I have not been to Antwerp before. We will have a great time."

"As usual the trip is yours to construct. Considering what the Germans did to Antwerp, I hope they left us a place to stay."

"I said I had never been to Antwerp. I did not say that members of my family did not do business there. I will see that you are comfortably housed and provisioned in the style to which you are accustomed my beloved," explained Aurora.

"I never doubted it for a minute," replied Cole.

Christmas at Aurora's home was an elaborate ritual. Neighbors not see since last Christmas were present at the series of Christmas concerts, dinners, and dances.

The house for weeks before Christmas day throbbed with activity. The servants went to great lengths to meet Aurora's expectations. The house was flawlessly cleaned and decorated exquisitely.

On Christmas day, the house was full of Aurora's oldest friends and her few remaining relatives. Because Cole and Aurora's year had gone well and Christmas had been a satisfying lengthy celebration, Cole was surprised that the day after Christmas, Aurora was in a funk which progressed throughout the day. He first attributed her low mood to fatigue but by the evening realized that other factors were at work.

"Can I ask what is wrong? You out did yourself this year. I hate to see you sad."

They sat in the library in a cozy corner where they usually worked in the evening.

"I miss having a child to share our happiness, our traditions. I assume that I have difficulty conceiving because of my condition. You know there were no children from my union with Marie-Henri, and I accepted that as part of what I had become.

"Eventually, I was glad there were none. Marie-Henri's deterioration was so profound that I realized that Marie-Henri would in time have corrupted our children. Perhaps, God protected me from that sorrow. But now I want us to have a child.

"Maybe medical science can help me, maybe God would show a doctor how to correct some flaw that is preventing conception? I know that I am much older than I appear and there may be no hope, but I want to try. Do you understand?" Aurora asked tearfully.

Cole bent over her chair and held her. "Of course, I understand. We can travel to Paris. One of the specialists there may be able to help us. There is no reason not to try. We can leave right away."

"No, I want to go to Antwerp first. I might become depressed if there is no hope. We should have a grand time first in Antwerp, with no worries there. Then we will go to Paris and fight for the possibility of a family."

Cole was surprised by Aurora's revelation. Their romance was new enough and their condition so unusual that he had not given much thought to the prospect of children. Once Aurora had declared that objective, Cole quickly realized that having children was something that he wanted as well.

He went to work to identify the top women's specialists in Paris. He wrote letters to the few French doctors who he knew or had heard of and asked for their recommendations.

Within a few weeks, he had several names and then set about contacting these men to see if they were the right ones to examine Aurora. Cole described Aurora as his fiancee and claimed she would not marry him unless she could give him children since she had been unable to conceive with her ex-husband and would not want to prevent Cole's happiness with another woman if she were indeed barren.

He counted on these male doctor's paternalistic prejudices to understand the logic of Aurora's supposed stipulation. Cole disliked the subterfuge but knew they otherwise would not accept Aurora as a patient, as an unmarried woman.

Of course, the simplest solution would be for them to marry, but Cole knew Aurora was hesitant to move forward with that at this time, due to the complexity of her estate and fear of Marie-Henri should he learn of her remarriage. After the encounter with Moreau on the train, Aurora had struggled with anxiety and constantly quizzed the servants on the security of the house.

While Cole pursued the details of the future Paris trip, Aurora worked with her contacts to arrange hotel rooms for them in Antwerp. Because the disclosure on the train had made her determined not to endure another disturbing encounter in close quarters, Aurora began to search for a suitable automobile for their trip to Antwerp.

Cole had been driving them to their weekly visit to the mental institution in a rickety roadster with the two of them swaddled in duster, gloves, hats, scarves, and goggles. It was a humiliating experience for them both.

Farmers at road side, pedestrians, passing motorists, all smiled or jeered as they clunked past, not too quickly, in their small open vehicle. Aurora wanted an appropriate vehicle for their trip to Belgium, but she also intended to put an end to nightmarish local trips during the day. She quickly learned that there were few reliable vehicles that met her requirements.

After much investigation, she finally found just the right car in a nearby town on the market because its previous owner had died recently and his heirs had no use for such an elaborate vehicle. The previous owner had purchased it new a few months before the war had begun, and Aurora had to hold her nose to conclude the transaction on a German built vehicle. Nonetheless, she had to admit that it was a beautiful beast, a splendid, spacious dark blue 1914 Mercedes open front town car. She intended to have one of the gardeners, who had been a driver during the war, act as chauffeur. He would sit in the open front, while they sat in the fully enclosed rear.

She began a lengthy modification of the car, replacing the windows in the passenger compartment with dark tinted glass and adding curtains and shades. Regardless of how bright the day, she and Cole could safely occupy the rear seat without worry. These modifications were expensive and time consuming so that the car was not ready for their trip for many months.

In August, they were finally ready to set out. They timed their departure to allow them to arrive at the border at sundown. Aurora did not want to attract attention by having to exit the vehicle in full sunlight covered like a burn victim.

The border guards were very curious about the vehicle and its contents but fortunately did not carefully examine the iced containers of liquid. From their polite smiles, Cole surmised that they viewed Aurora as another wealthy, eccentric French woman, one of many that they frequently encountered doing their job.

Their chauffeur, Paul, was an excellent driver and handled the bumpy, eroding roadway to Antwerp with considerable skill. Slow moving traffic, potholes, horse-drawn carts were all outmaneuvered with aplomb. They reached Antwerp late evening and were quickly escorted to their rooms on the same floor.

Aurora's room came with a sitting room and balcony with a beautiful view of the promenade and the Scheldt. After they unpacked, Aurora and Cole drank chilled blood and wine on the balcony, cooled by a sea breeze, while watching the boat traffic on the Scheldt. Eventually, they made love and slept well until dawn, when Cole returned to his room to avoid scandalizing the hotel staff.

In the morning, they set out on several excursions. Their driver left them at the entrance of their stops so that they could dash in without their usual complete coverage. They went to St. Paul's Church, the Cathedral of Our Lady, the Royal Museum of Fine Arts, and the Plantin-Moretus Museum.

Afterwards, they rested in Aurora's room before exiting at dusk for the Antwerp Zoo. They did not know if the zoo was open for an hour after sunset because it was late summer or because of the Olympics.

In any event, they counted themselves lucky to see a little of this remarkable zoo, one of the finest in Europe and one of the oldest in the world. They focused their attention on the Egyptian temple with its elephants and giraffes, the Moon temple with the Okapis, and the

Greek temple style reptile building. They hoped to return to see the Winter Garden and the Aquarium on a second visit later in the week.

The following day was the opening ceremony of the Games, and they had to endure the heat and the staring that came with the wearing of their protective clothing and eye wear. Aurora had seen that they were seated close to King Albert, who opened the Games, and she was ecstatic at the release of doves, a first for open ceremonies, to symbolize peace. She could barely constrain herself at the parade of athletes and lustily applauded the French participants as they passed her seat.

Unfortunately, she had so excited herself in the confining, hot clothing that she fell ill from the heat and they left early, returning to the hotel instead of going to the Gardens de la Palace d'Egmont to witness the fencing matches where they had hoped to witness the prowess of the remarkable Italian swordsman, Nedo Nadi.

In the hotel, they lay nude in Aurora's bed and gradually recovered from heat exhaustion, as they cooled slowly assisted by a slight breeze from the balcony. As the sun went down, they bathed and dressed for dinner. There was a centuries-old restaurant they wanted to experience, even if they could not really enjoy the full menu.

As usual, Aurora had arranged for them to have good seating in an excellent vantage point within the restaurant. As they entered, she took in the wide ornate fireplace, elaborate woodwork, and sweeping expanse of the ceiling, and did not notice that her entrance had elicited a commotion at a table near the center of the principal room.

Unfortunately, before Cole could alert her they were nearly even with the men at this table. Three men were standing all staring intently at Aurora. The tallest of the men glared at her and had malevolent, intense eyes that even to Cole were frightening to witness. Aurora had frozen in place when she saw the tall man and swayed and grasped Cole's hand. The tall man did not move but a muscular, well-dressed, mustached man bounded to their side.

"My dear Aurora, forgive me for being so forward but Marie-Henri has told me so much about you that I feel that I know you. When he just now spoke your name, I looked up and was overwhelmed at the accuracy of his description of you. Indeed, you are as beautiful as he has claimed ever so frequently.

"Please join our table, of course, with your companion. I am sure Marie-Henri would love to reminisce with you about your life together before the war. Oh, forgive me, let me introduce my very good friend, Eugene Bowling and, in my excitement, I realize I neglected to introduce myself. Baron Werner Gerbold at your service."

The Baron looked at Cole as if expecting an introduction. Cole did not want to have Aurora speak when she was struggling to contain herself.

"I am Cole Sterling, Baron. I am pleased to make your acquaintance, but I regret we will not be able to accept your kind invitation. Aurora has been ill and reluctantly agreed to accompany me to see the interior of this wonderful historic restaurant, but she appears to be relapsing. We will excuse ourselves. I hope you gentlemen have a pleasant evening."

Aurora turned away taking the arm of the manager who had been leading them deeper into the restaurant interior. He was an experienced older man and recognized the need for Madame to make an immediate retreat. As he led her back to the entrance, he could be heard loudly describing the history and special features of the elaborate interior.

Cole made a perfunctory nod of the head to the three men and followed Aurora and the manager to the door. Aurora gave the manager a large bank note from her evening bag along with a quick apology and strode into the humid night air gasping to catch her breath. Cole saw their car and signaled Paul, who brought the Mercedes to the curb.

"We are going back to the hotel but drive around for a while to make sure no one is following us," Cole ordered as he studied the restaurant entrance looking for Marie-Henri or any of the other men. A large party exited, obscuring his view of the door as they drove away.

"I am sorry Aurora. I know that encounter was disturbing for you. At least the good Inspector had given us some warning. I will try to telephone or telegraph him tomorrow about their presence here and will also visit the local police to see if there are arrest warrants pertaining to any of them within this country."

Aurora had her head pressed against the window glass, crying softly. Cole held her hand silently, respectfully allowing Aurora to reopen conversation when she was ready to express her feelings and fears about seeing Marie-Henri and the notorious Baron.

Cole's heart ached for her. She had looked forward to this trip, seeing it in part as a throwing off of her old sorrows. Now she was reliving the nightmare, with old wounds and fears re-exposed.

After a while, Paul did not see any suspicious vehicles following along their circuitous route back to the building, where he let them out at a side entrance to decrease chances of prying eyes noting their arrival. In the lobby, Aurora stopped Cole before they reached the elevators.

"I need some time alone in my room. Why don't you stay down here, have a drink in the bar, read the newspaper, smoke a foul cigar. Come to me in an hour. I do not want you watching me cry. I should be where I want to be in my mind when you come up, and we will talk then." She had given Cole a weak smile when she mentioned the foul cigar and she gave him another smile as she kissed him on the cheek before turning to the elevator.

Cole felt powerless as he watched her walk away. He shrugged, ambled over to the bar, ordered a brandy, and sat at a small corner table when he sipped his drink and reviewed a wrinkled copy of the daily paper, which as expected was full of news about the Olympics. He watched an ornate clock on the wall until 45 minutes had passed, which was as long as he could endure away from Aurora. He strolled to the elevator and gave the operator his floor.

"That is a busy floor tonight. A few minutes, ago, the manager, assistant manager, and house detective went up, and I just now brought up some police."

"Do you know what is wrong?" asked Cole anxiously.

"I wish. It will be a while before the hotel gossips get around to telling me anything. Well, here is your floor."

Cole stepped out of the elevator apprehensively and caught his breath at the sight of two men standing at the door of Aurora's room. He sprinted down the hall. A weary looking policeman held up his arm to stop Cole. A diminutive man whispered in the policeman's ear, and he stepped aside to let Cole enter the suite. At the door, the little man caught Cole's arm and said, "Brace yourself, Sir."

Cole entered the suite shakily, forcing himself to slowly make his way from the atrium to where a small group of men were gathered around a figure on the floor next to the balcony door.

Aurora lay in a pool of blood still dressed in her evening clothes. The men moved aside as he approached. Aurora was on her side and had bled from a wound in her back likely sustained as she fled from her assailant. The blood had drained in the direction of her feet, leaving her beautiful profile framed by long hair untouched. She looked asleep.

Cole fell to his knees next to her face and placed his head against hers as he sobbed. He had no idea how long he stayed that way before finally a soft voice said, "You need to go, Sir. We have to do our work. I know you would want us to do that."

Strong arms gently pulled him upright. Cole swayed

on his feet and wiped the tears from his eyes as he realized that he was facing the view of the Scheldt from the balcony.

A luxurious riverboat was passing through a fine fog. People were dancing to waltz music, which carried clearly over the water along with the sound of people chattering and laughing. A man and women in fine evening dress leaned contentedly against the rail of the boat just as a billow of fog reached out and snatched them from view.

"Come, Sir, it is time to go," whispered the gentle voice, as Cole was pulled away from where he stood next to Aurora.

PART TWO

KNOXVILLE, TENNESSEE

1922

From his upstairs study, Cole had watched the petite young woman clad in men's work clothes hammering stakes in some sort of pattern in the grass of the gently sloping backyard of the house adjacent to his.

The sun had just sat and he observed her through his dark glasses as the sunlight dwindled down to where he could exit the house without appearing dressed for polar exploration. He ambled over to where the woman was now feverishly digging a hole at one of the sites she had previously marked.

She started when he asked, "Have you begun a great archeological dig? I am certainly impressed by the scope of the project."

"Go ahead, make fun of me, everyone else does. There is no reason a complete stranger should not have fun at my expense," said the young woman, scowling up at Cole as she smeared dirt across her forehead as she wiped away perspiration with the back of her hand.

"I apologize, Miss, for startling you and for being overly familiar. I am Dr. Sterling, your new neighbor. I was attempting a little humor and, indeed, there was so little humor there was none. I don't mean to intrude. I really came over to introduce myself."

"I have seen you once from a distance. You were bundled up in all this heat like it was January. I thought you might be a frail old man but here you are neither old or frail," the girl observed.

"I have a disorder that prevents me from having any sun exposure. I rarely venture outside except after sundown. When I must go out in the day, I look most odd, covered from head to toe, to people who do not know me. I dislike living in the shadows and could not resist leaving the confines of my house tonight as soon as I could safely do so," Cole replied.

"I have never heard of anyone made ill by the sun. Most ladies protect their skin from the sun. They do not want to look like field hands, but sick from the sun, that is new to me," she said.

"There are several diseases where the sun is not tolerated, lupus erythematosus, for example, but my disorder is very rare, nearly unique. I keep hoping I will improve but I do not," said Cole.

"I am sorry to hear that but getting back to your

initial question, my project is to plant the 13 sacred trees of the Celts, well they are not all trees but most are. I am laying them out in a ellipse running down the hill. The pattern is marked and I am digging my first hole before my mother gets home. If I get well started I have a better chance of her not hollering at me and making me pull the stakes out," the girl explained.

"You did not ask her before you started?" said Cole.

"If you knew my mother, you would know that this is the only way I might succeed in getting the trees planted," said the girl.

"Why do you want sacred trees of Celts on your property?" asked Cole. "Are they good luck or prevent some particular misfortune?"

"I went to a private girl's school and my favorite teacher taught us about the Celts, their myths and religion, and I became interested in their culture. After graduation, I went to New York to study with my aunt for a while, trying to decide if I wanted to go to college or find an occupation. I spent a lot of time in the public library there. They have many books on the Celts, and I decided I wanted the 13 sacred trees of the Celts. I intend to sit in the center of the ellipse and see if I sense anything different," she explained.

"That sounds like an interesting experiment, Miss, but you might have to try it at different times, full moon, different seasons, that sort of thing," said Cole.

"I am Catherine, Dr. Sterling, most people around here would talk to me like I am touched. You do not seem to be humoring me," Catherine observed.

"Well, Catherine, the good news is even if the reality does not line up to your expectations, the center of your ellipse seems like a good place to be on the grass and gaze up at the stars on a clear night," replied Cole.

Catherine laughed, "You are a practical man, Dr. Sterling, in your view even if I do not have a transcendent spiritual experience at least I have a pleasant place to lollygag."

"I am a fount of wisdom, but life has already taught me that well-laid plans often go astray and we have to seize the remaining opportunities that present themselves. Watching the stars swim by on a beautiful night might be a sort of transcendent spiritual experience. One that we should not miss," Cole said.

Catherine looked at a time piece in her pocket and said, "You must excuse me, Dr. Sterling, my mother will be home any minute now, and I want to clean up before she sees me. Getting caught in the act is probably not a good idea."

Catherine moved towards her home and then turned back to Cole. "My mother wants to invite you for dinner, to welcome you here. I will tell her I have met you and why we do not see much of you. I will come by with a specific invitation from her."

"I would love that, Catherine, I would like to join you but, in order not to risk offending your mother, you should know I eat very little; I am primarily a vegetarian, although occasionally I eat a little fish. After my illness, I cannot eat meat and I cannot eat much at one time. I would enjoy your company, but your mother should not concern herself with my meal," Cole said.

"We will invite you for one of my mother's usual suppers. There will be plenty of vegetables and my family will certainly make up for your forbearance with food consumption," said Catherine.

"Good night, Catherine, it was a pleasure to talk to you," said Cole. Catherine waved and marched off to the basement storage room with her shovel over her shoulder.

Cole sat in an armchair at the edge of his desk with his notepad in his lap and watched as the woman on the settee across from him gazed around his office.

"I thought psychoanalysts had an analyst couch where patients reclined," said Mrs. Lear.

"Many do. I have a number of women in my practice. Some might find it intimidating to recline in the presence of someone who is a stranger. Women or men, some individuals might see an element of subservience in reclining with someone peering over them. Besides, I have businessmen patients who would find it hard to resist a good nap," laughed Cole.

Mrs. Lear did not seem particularly amused at the thought of drowsy men sharing the consult room and continued to examine his office.

"Why do you have colored glass windows in here? It reminds me of a minister's office in a very old church. I am not a very religious person. I hope there is not a religious theme to your practice. I want scientific medical guidance, not clerical dogma," she noted sternly.

"I assure you I offer modern secular psychoanalysis. The windows filter the sun for me. I cannot tolerate direct sunlight and it seems less gloomy in her with the filtered light, instead of having imposing heavy drapes on the windows," said Cole. "Can you tell me about yourself, Mrs. Lear," he continued, trying to redirect the conversation to a more productive direction.

"Do you mind if I smoke; it relaxes me?" asked Mrs. Lear.

"No, not at all, there is an ashtray over there," he indicated with a wave of his hand.

Mrs. Lear lit her cigarette and paced the room before beginning her story. Cole could assess her better as she strolled about his office. She was an elegant woman, well but conservatively dressed. The cigarette did seem to relax her; her tone was subdued when she spoke again.

"I need to learn to meet my husband's expectations. He is a minister, which is why I reacted to your stained-glass windows I suppose. To the world at large he appears to be a wonderful warm man, beloved for his good works in the community, seemingly a good father and an inspiring minister, but he has a different face at home.

"I never seem to satisfy him. I am expected to participate in most church activities and to lead with women's groups and he is never satisfied. No matter what I do it is not enough.

"Edgar, my husband, is foul-tempered and I can never please him with anything I do. He has always spent a lot of time with our daughter but now I am excluded. They have a special bond and I feel my presence resented," Mrs. Lear paused and stared at Cole.

"But there must be something wrong with me to feel this way. They are my husband and daughter. Am I being paranoid? I am afraid that I do not see things as they really are, that I am making stupid mistakes and that I have done something to drive my husband and daughter away," tears welled in Mrs. Lear's eyes and her hands trembled such that the long ash from her neglected cigarette fell to the carpet.

Cole left his chair and gently guided her to a winged-back chair where she curled tightly into a corner of the soft leather.

"I understand you are struggling with your emotions right now. I do not want to pursue the details of the problems you are having at home. We will continue that at your next visit. Before you leave today, I want to explore your earlier life so that I understand the woman who sits before me. It is important to understand you, your personality, early experiences, and belief system, if I am to help you with your present difficulties," said Cole.

Mrs. Lear sniffed and nodded her head in agreement. Cole elicited a history of her childhood and and noted that she had a happy upbringing with kind, loving parents, and supportive friends. As she reviewed her early life, Mrs. Lear smiled and seemed comfortable with her memories. She denied any early traumas or abuse and appeared mildly shocked that he would even ask such things. She was also bright and cheerful discussing her courtship by the young minister, who became her husband.

Cole decided to stop on a positive emotional note and ended the session with a pleasant recollection of her wedding and honeymoon. He told her they would move forward in time from there at her next visit.

As he escorted her to the door, he said, "Oh, there is one small thing. You said your husband was seemingly a good father. I could not help but wonder what you meant by saying 'seemingly.' Is he less than he should be as a father?"

This caught Mrs. Lear off guard, as he knew it would, and she flushed and was momentarily at a loss for words. She stammered, "I did not realize I said 'seemingly.' He is a good father but I worry that his and my daughter's closeness interferes with the rest of her life."

Mrs. Lear did not look at Cole as she slipped out of the door and said softly as she walked away, "It is unnatural for a young girl to be so preoccupied and attentive to her father."

Cole watched her as his secretary escorted her to the outside door. Her previous ebullient mood had flicked out at the first mention of her husband's relationship with her daughter.

Catherine met Cole at the front door and smilingly led him into the parlor where she offered him lemonade or iced tea. Catherine poured him a generous glass of the tea he had selected from a frosted pitcher resting on a wonderfully ornate, oak side table.

"Supper will be ready right away and, just in time to join us, here is my usually perpetually tardy father," said Catherine as she kissed a burly dark-haired man Cole would never have guessed was the father of petite Catherine.

"Catherine has rattled on about you quite a bit Dr. Sterling, it is a pleasure to meet you finally. I am Jake Wainwright and I welcome you to our home."

Cole shook hands with Jake as they both insisted the other use his first name.

Catherine is a sound judge of character, unlike my other daughter, so I felt secure in having you to supper tonight," said Jake. "I do not think I could have survived another evening with some of the radical layabouts Clover cultivates," said Jake.

A silky voice intruded, "My friends are not radical, Father, they are progressive and they have an expansive view of the world and engage in sophisticated, witty banter. No doubt they find your provincial conversation as tedious as you find theirs."

Cole could not help smiling at the raven-haired beauty before him. The father's commanding presence had been transferred to this daughter along with his dark hair.

Jake rolled his eyes and, gesturing at Clover, asked if Cole had met his oldest daughter.

"No, but I am delighted to meet you, Clover, call me Cole."

Clover appraised him from shoes to hair before pronouncing, "You are as debonair as Catherine said. You must have an active practice of neurotic ladies eager to confess their troubles lying on your psychiatrist's couch."

"Oh, Clover, that verges on the vulgar. I apologize for my sister, she usually endeavors to be shocking and usually succeeds," said Catherine.

Cole laughed, "Actually, I do not have a psychiatrist's couch in my office, in spite of the popular image of psychiatry. I find people can talk to me just fine with both feet on the floor."

At this point, the girl's mother, Constance, walked in announcing supper. She and Cole were introduced and the group sauntered into the dining room, where a large mahogany table was replete with serving dishes of collard greens, cabbage, fried okra, mashed potatoes, black-eyed peas, and green beans, surrounding a succulent ham next to a platter of golden brown corn bread. After the party had been served, Cole made a point of mentioning to Constance that the small portions he had taken were due to his disability, not a reflection of her cooking.

"Catherine told me you did not eat much and avoided meat, so we have a plethora of good Southern vegetables tonight. Most of the cooking is done by our wonderful cook, Mable, who is a treasure and invaluable since neither of my daughters have an interest in cooking," said Constance.

"Too much education and too modern," snorted Jake. "If they ever marry, which is uncertain, I suspect their husbands and children will wither away."

"A modern woman has interests other than feeding men and procreating, Father dear," said Clover. "There are social injustices to correct, promotion of the arts, and working for world peace and a community of nations."

Jake looked at Cole and said, "Clover is rather naive about the way the world works and certainly does not understand the problems of the American businessman. I hope with time that she will expand her views of these things, but for now I will just be happy if I don't get a late-night call informing me of her arrest at a speakeasy."

Clover glared at her father venomously. "Any police carrying me away might be eager to hear of your cache of single malt whiskey and French wine hidden away in the basement."

Jake laughed. "All the more reason to hope you don't go off in a Black Maria. You obviously would not stand up before a tough police billy club and bright lights."

Constance spoke with mock seriousness, "Well, Dr. Sterling, I guess the illusion of my family as hard working, staunch teetotalers is shattered. At least now, due to my overly vocal daughter, I will be able to offer you a bit of brandy in your coffee with dessert. I hope you will keep my family's moral failings from the general public."

Cole smiled and said, "A physician is used to confidences. I am well practiced at being discreet and, yes, a mite of brandy with coffee later would be well received. Sinful liquor has not passed my lips in quite a while now."

"I have some Cuban cigars for our coffee. We better smoke them before they are outlawed, too," said Jake with a chortle.

"Sounds splendid," said Cole

Jake took over the table conversation at this point and gave Cole the rundown on business conditions and politics in Knoxville. As a manufacturer, he was knowledgeable about anything in Knoxville and the State of Tennessee that might affect his business.

When Jake seemed to be losing steam, Constance jumped in with her review of social and cultural strengths in Knoxville. Cole noticed that she did not say much about the social problems that even a casual observer would discern. Before Cole could ask her about this, Constance changed conversation paths and asked Cole about his practice.

"I was originally a surgeon," he said. "But my war injuries finished that as a carrier path. Fortunately, the woman who saw to my recovery was a lay psychoanalyst and convinced me to focus on psychiatry. Originally, I concentrated on soldiers struggling with neurasthenia from the horrors and terror they found in combat. That is still a significant part of my present practice, but I have expanded to anyone with troubles of the mind. I have been attempting to help to educate the local general practitioners that I can also be of help to any of their patients whose mental outlook interferes with their ability to work, love, or play."

Cole laughed. "I have not been very successful at this. The Protestant work ethic is strong here as is the concept that life is a veil of tears. Even convincing educated physicians that our patients can be assisted with their mental adaptation to life's trials and tribulations is challenging."

"You do have your work cut out for you, Cole. Most

folks around here would consult their minister, not a doctor, for their problems," said Constance.

"I understand, but I hope to educate everyone that medical and spiritual advice are not only not incompatible, but in many cases, can work together to solve patient problems. There is a lot of silent anguish that can be alleviated," Cole said.

"Speaking of silent anguish, I will cure mine by excusing myself to attend a previously arranged engagement," said Clover as she stood and walked over to Cole's chair.

Cole stood and took Clover's proferred hand.

She said, "I hope to see you often Cole. I can be an informative guide to the Knoxville my parents have not discussed. Good evening."

As Clover exited the room, Cole saw that Jake's complexion was now a bright red and Constance looked pale and stunned.

Catherine rose quickly from her seat and said, "Lets adjourn to the parlor, everyone. Cole, you and Dad, go in. Mother and I will be in with coffee and those cigars Dad mentioned."

The older man seemed reluctant to leave his seat, but slowly pushed his chair away from the table and led Cole back into the parlor to await Constance and Catherine.

Cole probed Jake for details of his business in order to avoid any further mention of Clover. Jake was taciturn at first but warmed to his exposition, clearly proud of the growth of the glove manufacturing facility he and his father had started two decades ago. He described how they controlled the process from the preparation of the leather to the design and manufacture of men and women's fine fashion gloves, as well as a multitude of work gloves for different occupations.

Catherine returned with a tray of coffee for the men and overheard the end of her father's comments.

"We are proud of the plant and its products, but Clover and I tire of being reminded we are not strapping young fellows who can take over from Dad. Unfortunately for him, neither of us seem very likely to marry the perfect hardworking son-in-law for him to train as his successor," said Catherine.

She kissed her father on his head and said, "I suppose he will have to keep his nose to the grindstone for now and find his own successor at the plant."

Jake good-naturedly patted Catherine's hand and said, "I have not given up on you, Catherine. The plant management needs to stay with family. We will persevere. We always have." Jake spiked their coffee with brandy and passed a fragrant Cuban cigar to Cole.

"Mother sends her regrets, Cole. She has a headache and is retiring early," said Catherine.

"Please tell your mother how much I enjoyed our food and the company this evening," said Cole.

Jake was flushed again and was clearly struggling to not say anything. To temper his discomfort, Cole began to ask questions about leather tanning and how they graded the product.

Cole could see that Catherine was pleased at his deft handling of her father's embarrassment and interjected a few comments of her own to keep the conversation on mundane topics.

She managed to get Jake off on a discourse about UT Football and Jake quickly forgot any social embarrassment he had suffered. After a reasonable time, Cole felt that he could go home without Jake concluding that Cole had been run off by his family's less than gracious behavior. Cole thanked Jake sincerely for the dinner and cigar and allowed Catherine to walk him to the door.

When she knew Jake could not overhear, Catherine began to speak. "Thanks for managing my father so well. He works very hard for his family and is a dear. My sister is quite a thorn in his side. She has always been strong-willed and a bit of a princess.

"She embraced all the new ideas about women in society as a justification for her approach to life. Mother is not strong enough to cope with her, and my father is both worried for her and chagrined at how her behavior reflects on our family. Clover pontificates about the new woman improving society, but most of her time is spent on late night rambling with dubious friends."

Catherine grinned and continued, "I do envy her some. Some of her questionable friends are quite handsome and a few have money. She could surprise us all and marry a banker's son."

Cole smiled and said, "You are quite a force yourself, Catherine, and very pretty. Clover may end up attracting the wrong sort of man. I think that your father understands that you will choose well and wisely."

Cole clasped her hand and said, "Good evening,

Catherine, I have enjoyed it wholeheartedly. Thanks for inviting me."

As he left the doorway, Cole could see that Catherine was still blushing and for once speechless.

~

Cole became increasingly concerned in his sessions with Mrs. Lear.

He had convinced himself that she was not troubled by her own inner life but was agitated by the relationship of her husband and daughter. She could not consciously frame her suspicions regarding her husband and instead focused on his admittedly boorish behavior. She still looked for an answer that would come from a change in herself, an as yet, unrecognized modification of her behavior that would ameliorate the problem.

Cole had gently tried to get Mrs. Lear to confront the possibility of her daughter's abuse, but was blocked by her resistance to this idea and could not develop this concept without driving her away. After their last session, he was determined to visit the Reverend Lear. He did not tell Mrs. Lear of his plan, and while acknowledging the impropriety of this contact, could not ignore the implications of his continued inaction on the fate of the Lear daughter.

From his sessions, Cole had made note that the Reverend habitually worked on his sermons on Tuesday evenings while Mrs. Lear and her daughter visited family and friends.

As he left to drive to the Lear's home at the outskirts

of town, a furious blowing rain began to pelt his car. The cloudy, moonless night made it difficult to find the Lear residence, which happened to be a solitary house at the end of a lengthy curvy dirt path, now a muddy shallow stream from the downpour.

Cole parked his car under a heavy canopy of oaks on a slight elevation off the road a few yards from the Lear's drive. He kept a black, rubberized, hooded rain garb in his car for this type of situation, and after slipping this on, trudged carefully over to the Lear house.

Cole's enhanced night vision allowed him to walk to the house by staying at the edge of the adjoined woods and avoiding the worst of the flooding. He ended up on the Lear porch without appreciable mud on his boots. After slipping off the rain gear, Cole knocked on the front door.

Reverend Lear was slow to answer the door, possibly due to the sound of knocking being obscured by the thunder and the clatter of rain, or from reluctance to answer the door to an unexpected visitor on such a night. When his face appeared at the crack in the door, he scowled suspiciously at his visitor.

"Reverend Lear, I am Dr. Sterling, your wife's physician. May I speak with you," said Cole.

Reverend Lear's demeanor did not change with Cole identifying himself.

"What do you want," he demanded without asking Cole inside.

"Well, I have important issues to discuss. May I come in? I will not take a lot of your time."

Reverend Lear hesitated but then, with obvious

reluctance, opened the door for Cole. He stalked off to the room where he had been working without a word, expecting Cole to follow along.

Reverend Lear's study was vibrant. Full of books and colorful mementos from what Cole speculated were missionary trips to South America. A bull whip with an ornate silver handle decorated the fireplace mantle and a cowboy six-shooter hung on pegs above the whip.

"You have a very pleasant study," said Cole.

Reverend Lear plopped down behind his desk, which was busy with scattered notes and open books. He ignored Cole's effort at introductory pleasantries and said again, "What do you want?"

Cole had not been asked to sit but seated himself in a straight-back chair closest to Reverend Lear. "As you may know, your wife came to me ostensibly to help her with possible feelings that prevented her from pleasing you. With time, I realized that she was unlikely to be the primary problem. In fact, your relationship with your daughter clearly was interfering with your relationship with your wife.

"Your wife is suppressing the full implications of the details she is relating to me. I think she came to me not because she believed you and your daughter's relationship to be abnormally close, but because she, at some level, knows that your relationship is incestuous."

"How dare you come to me with this drivel. Your patron saint is that sexual deviant Freud and you appear here without any proof of your accusations," said Reverend Lear.

"If I had proof, the sheriff would be here, not me. I

came here because I want you to stop before your daughter is destroyed. You believe in redemption. This is your chance. There will not be another. I do not expect you to confess your sins to me. I do insist you terminate your sinful actions against your daughter immediately," said Cole.

"I will report you to the medical board for coming this way and making unsupported slanderous accusations," said Reverend Lear.

"Do what you must. I assure you, all the appropriate authorities will know about you if you fail to change your behavior," warned Cole as he rose from the chair and turned to walk back to the front door.

A biting sting sliced across the back of his neck, causing Cole to lose his balance and topple onto the floor. As he turned over he saw Reverend Lear drop the bullwhip and level the pistol from the mantel at his chest. Cole pivoted to his left as Reverend Lear fired, the bullet burrowed into the floor less than an inch from his shoulder.

Reverend Lear had a look of incredulity on his face seeing the speed with which Cole moved from the floor to his side. Cole pushed the pistol barrel upward as Reverend Lear pulled the trigger again, firing a bullet into his neck which came out the back of his skull.

The report was deafening and Cole released Reverend Lear to slide to the floor, where he writhed with blood gushing over the floor and Cole's feet. Cole was at first transfixed by the pulsing crimson stream, but then fell to his knees, covering the gaping wound on

Lear's neck with his mouth, gulping the torrent of delicious liquid until the flow was a mere trickle.

As suddenly as he had begun to drink, he now ended, throwing the blood drained corpse against the wall and rolling back on his buttocks. After a few seconds, he stood and surveyed the carnage that had transformed the previously serene room. His disgust at the gory scene was nothing in comparison to the revulsion exploding inside of him as his mind confronted the reality of what he had just done.

He walked out of the house as he had come in, retrieving his rain gear at the door and striding off into the adjacent dark woods. He quickly found his car and retrieved overalls and work shoes he kept for roadside repairs.

In the shadows, he stripped off his bloody clothing and shoes, including the driving gloves he had fortunately worn, and rolled them all inside the raincoat and tied it in a bundle with several large stones from the ground as ballast.

As horrified as Cole was by his ghoulish actions, he had no intention of accepting any blame for the death of the repugnant Reverend Lear. He drove off for home while considering the best place to dump the incriminating articles. Cole decided to find an isolated bank of the Tennessee River and sat out along a route that would bring him near the river.

After a while, his mind began to struggle with the horror that would await Mrs. Lear and her daughter when they entered their house. He had intervened to interrupt the victimization of the Lear daughter and now he had added to the deep psychic scars she would carry for the remainder of her life.

He determined to try to prevent the daughter from seeing her father's body in this fashion. Fortunately, the rain had stopped and Cole began to look for an open business where he might be able to access a telephone.

Just before he came near the river, there was a mechanic's garage beside the road and he pulled over in a dark spot about fifty yards from the building. No one was around the outside of the garage as he approached it.

Inside the open front of the structure, a lone man was underneath an old battered automobile that might better belong in a junk yard than receiving the ministrations of a greasy mechanic. Cole saw nor sensed anyone else nearby. He slipped into the grimy small office at the front of the building and was relieved to see a telephone.

He asked the operator for the police department, and speaking into the receiver through a stained rag from the counter, he announced the need to go immediately to Reverend Lear's house, where he had shot himself. With that, he quietly exited the office and quickly faded into the night as he returned to his car.

At the river bank , he cautiously parked and went some distance from the car before he found the right spot for disposing of the bundle. His remarkable night vision allowed him to confirm that no one else was nearby. Any night anglers would have fled the intense rain earlier in the evening.

Cole swung the bundle back and forth several times until he was able to sling it with considerable force out into the main channel of the river where it sunk straightaway. Back in his car, Cole realized he was covered with sweat and was trembling. He fought to control himself as he drove home to avoid appearing intoxicated to any lurking police he might pass.

Once home, he stripped and carefully examined his work clothes but failed to find traces of blood and left them for washing by the cleaning lady. He took a strong bromide and savored a warm bath while he waited for the drug to manifest its effects.

He finally fell into bed naked and still damp from the cursory toweling of his now languid hands. Cole slept without dreams until he heard his secretary enter the house the next morning. He quickly dressed and rushed downstairs to be prepared for his first patient.

Eveline, his secretary and receptionist, was listing to WNOX as he came into the room. Her face was ashen and her eyes were watering.

"Doctor, they are saying on the radio that Reverend Lear is dead at his home from a gunshot. The police are investigating," said Eveline.

"Was his family there?" asked Cole.

"I don't know, that is really all they said," Eveline replied.

"When was Mrs. Lear to be back with me?" Cole asked.

"Not until next week. Oh, how horrible for her and her daughter. What on earth could have happened?"

Cole's first patient of the day came in before Cole could reply, for which he was most grateful. Cole escorted the teary matron into his office himself, where he made every effort to devote his intellect entirely to her service. Cole knew that he could not avoid ruminating on his actions and potential consequences, but for now he was in the familiar role of diagnosing and treating the troubles of the mind in his patients. His problems and anguish would have to wait.

Cole sent a condolence note to Mrs. Lear, and a few days later received a brief letter from her thanking him for helping her to gain self-confidence and to see her relationship with her deceased husband in a different light.

She went on to say that she and her daughter were moving to Nashville to stay with relatives and rebuild their lives in a place not filled by old difficult memories. Mrs. Lear did not allude to the circumstances of her husband's death.

Cole continued to alternate between guilt and feeling of heightened power and exhilaration. The human blood he had drunk made him surge with energy and vibrancy. His patients and secretary all commented on his transformation. Previously, he had seemed bookish in appearance, pale and fragile. Now his complexion was ruddy, his movements confident and deliberate, and he joked and smiled.

He now looked like the young surgeon who had gone off to support his country's war in Europe. Soon after Aurora had died, Cole had lost access to human blood and had sustained himself entirely on animal blood.

Here in Knoxville he readily obtained the blood of freshly slaughtered cows and had made no effort to locate human blood. The potential pitfalls of seeking human blood through various ruses were troubling and, up to now, had not seemed worthwhile. The torpor from long-term deprivation of human blood had fogged his mind to the resulting vitiation of his life force. He now understood that he would have to confront his need for human blood and seek a regular source.

~

Two days after receiving Mrs. Lear's letter, Cole had a visit from the police. A detective had scheduled an appointment with him at the end of his work day and strolled into Cole's consultation room with the air of a man so in touch with this world's realities, that he could quickly locate the small secretive spider spinning its web in an occult crevice or a man, fallen from God's grace, with a horrible secret buried in his breast.

Cole chilled at the sight of Detective Ross, six feet, powerfully built, and surprising well dressed in an expensive suit. Ross surveyed Cole and his office with a few quick glances. Ross stood in the center of the room with his hat in his hand for a few seconds before Cole caught himself and asked the detective to take a seat.

"I am sorry to bother you, Dr. Sterling, but I need to make a few inquiries. I understand the recently deceased Reverend Lear's wife is your patient," said Detective Ross.

"Patients have doctor-patient confidentially. I really can't discuss Mrs. Lear," said Cole.

"Mrs. Lear told me she consulted you and had no

objection to my talking to you, as this is a police investigation of a possible crime," said Detective Ross.

"A crime? I heard a rumor of suicide," said Cole.

"I cannot discuss the circumstances but it appears that someone was with Reverend Lear at the time of his death," Detective Ross explained.

"With him or harmed him?" asked Cole.

"That's our dilemma. We are still investigating."

"I do not see how I can help you with that, and I cannot discuss Mrs. Lear's reasons for consulting me, but I have no problem in stating unequivocally that she revealed no violent tendencies and never expressed a desire to directly or indirectly harm her husband," said Cole.

"Did she ever mention anyone who was in conflict with her or her husband," said Detective Ross.

"I have no recollection of anything like that," said Cole.

"Where were you the night he died?" asked Detective Ross.

"Why would you ask that? I never met the man," Cole responded.

"Detectives see a lot of sordidness. Mrs. Lear is an attractive woman, unhappy about something, and she confides in you a young doctor home from the war. Intimate relationships have spawned with less opportunity," replied Detective Ross.

"I have many reasons to be indignant at that implication, Detective. I choose not to be angry because of your need to explore possibilities. Simply put, Mrs. Lear and I had a professional relationship, nothing else," Cole said.

"Then you won't mind telling me of your whereabouts that night," said Detective Ross.

"I was home. I went out in my car to go downtown to a booksellers shop but a hard rain developed, and I turned around and came home," said Cole.

"Can anyone confirm that?" asked Detective Ross.

"No, I live alone. I have a friend in Nashville who often stays here when he has business in these parts, but he has not been here in weeks," answered Cole.

"Can you think of anything that would help my investigation?" asked Detective Ross.

"No, absolutely nothing," said Cole.

"Well, I will move on, then. If you think of anything I should know, call me. Your secretary has my number."

The detective and Cole crossed to the door, when Ross planted his hat firmly on his head and shook Cole's hand.

"For Mrs. Lear's sake, I have to ask what the odds are that you will be able to give her a definite answer to the circumstances of her husband's death," asked Cole.

Ross looked rather sinister with the brim of his hat pulled down, shadowing his eyes.

"A criminal often gives himself away. Guilt is powerful. A man knows what he did and his anxiety leads him to make mistakes and create suspicions that draw us to him," Detective Ross said.

"A man may not always know what he did, Detective. In psychiatry we are familiar with such things. A simple example is the alcoholic with blackouts. Such men may not suspect they have committed a crime. Your theory would break down here," countered Cole.

Detective Ross stared intensely at Cole for several seconds before saying, "A very interesting observation, Doctor."

He turned and followed Cole's secretary to the outside door. Cole watched him exit and thought, *Detective, you may be more correct than you know. If I were not anxious, I would not have antagonized you circumspectly with my intuition about your alcoholic blackouts.*

Cole sat in a wingback chair and berated himself for his comment. Now he made Detective Ross intensely interested in him as a person, if not a suspect. A man like Ross would now move heaven and earth to try to figure out how Cole might have suspected such a flaw in his character. Cole did not know why his intuitions about people were growing stronger with time. They had started after his transformation and became clearer with the passage of time.

Aurora had confirmed that the same had occurred with her but she had not developed the clarity that Cole was evolving. His intuitions about people were especially useful in his practice and he opened himself to this mysterious ability. In fact, this extra source of information was what had made him confident that Reverend Lear was a child molester. Now, for the first time, he had slipped and said something to someone that would make the person curious about how Cole had knowledge of a personal secret.

∽

The evening of the same day as Detective Ross's visit, Cole answered his door to find Clover standing before him in a flimsy, short red dress, loose stockings pulled to her knees, and her luxuriant hair cropped to frame her face.

"Don't just stand there looking like you have been poleaxed. Invite me in," she said.

Cole blushed and hurriedly brought her inside.

"I'm sorry, the change in your appearance is striking. I'm surprised," said Cole.

"You obviously do not look at fashionable magazines. This is how young women dress these days and, if you were not a gad, you would have told me how beautiful I am with my new look," replied Clover.

"You were beautiful and elegant when I met you, Clover, and you are beautiful and stunning now," said Cole.

Clover laughed. "I was not seriously looking for compliments, Cole, but that is your problem, you are much too serious. That's why I am here. I am taking you dancing tonight."

Cole looked down at his worn business suit. "Do I need to change?"

"When you have me with you, there is nothing else you could possibly need. Let's go," said Clover.

Cole barely grabbed his hat before Clover had him outside. Clover directed Cole as they drove in his car outside town. She spent half the trip condemning his automobile and insisting that he visit a family friend with a car dealership who would get him a more suitable vehicle.

Cole was happy to see their destination, a flat roof block-like building off by itself, away from the highway. He liked his Ford and was not enthusiastic at the prospect of parting with it.

"What an odd building," Cole said.

"The larger opening in front is where you place your order, pass money, and they hand over your booze. It is small so you can't get too threatening through that small opening. All the little slits along that wall are gun ports," said Clover.

"You are serious?" asked Cole.

"There are a lot of people, on both sides of the law, who want the owner's liquor and his money. They would probably put in a moat if they thought it would do them any good. Park on the side. We go in there," said Clover.

A small dirt parking area on the entrance side of the building was full of both decrepit and new sleek automobiles. Cole found a small area where he hoped he would not get dinged by departing drinkers and followed Clover to the formidable door, which appeared to be the only entrance into this quasi-military outpost.

Clover banged loudly on the door with a staccato rhythm, but that Cole surmised was an entrance code. They must have passed muster viewed through the peephole since the door moved enough to let them squeeze through into a vestibule where two men were standing. They did not look particularly friendly, but had recognized Clover and were giving her what they probably intended as warm smiles, which Cole seriously doubted had even a glimmer of genuine human warmth.

"So, Clover, you brought a friend," stated the taller

man, with the eyes and smile that could easily win any most reptilian contest.

"This is my neighbor, Dr. Sterling, John. I thought I would show him a good time tonight. He does not get out much," replied Clover.

John shook Cole's hand with a firmness that Cole suspected was a silent warning of the force that John could bring to bear on anyone he decided had overstepped their bounds in his speakeasy.

Cole pretended to wince with John's grasp. He had a long-standing rule of allowing the insignificant self-important the perpetuation of their delusion of omnipotence.

John was apparently not in the mood for small talk and handily opened another heavy door to admit them into a smoky cavern where Cole was buffeted with the pounding, syncopated harmonious delivery of a jazz quartet. A crowded dance floor in front of the band pulsated with sweaty, inebriated denizens, most of whom were displaying only rudimentary knowledge of the dance they were performing.

Cole was drug by Clover to a table off in a corner, when two bleary-eyed men sat.

"Ah, Clover, come save us from the tedium of this dreary establishment. Who is this chap? A new playmate?" said the thinner of the two men with a distinct English accent.

Both men half rose from their chairs and switched their cigarettes to their left hands to permit Cole to shake their hands. They seemed a bit unsteady and Cole doubted they could have easily risen completely from their seats.

Clover introduced Cole and then presented her two friends to him. The Englishman was Alexander Forester and had some sort of job in banking. The other man, Bill Pine, was in insurance and was a Tennessean. Cole sensed that both men had been in the war and they seemed good sorts, although deep in their cups tonight.

Clover knew Alexander and Bill were too far gone to attempt conversation and ordered them to flag a waiter to extract libations for herself and Cole. She pulled Cole out among the would-be dancers and berated him as she struggled to show him the foxtrot.

As the band changed music, Clover transformed Cole to a sweat-swathed scarecrow as she pushed him from one dance form to the next. Finally, Clover tired and lead him back to the table where Alexander and Bill ruminated.

"I thought you did bloody well, Cole. Clover did not reduce you to tears and no one out there took a shot at you. A rather successful campaign I would say," pronounced Alexander with greater clarity than Cole would have expected, based on his overall condition. Clover tossed back her drink and strolled off to find the powder room.

Cole regarded his glass with a jaundiced eye. Alexander spoke up, "No problem, old boy, we drink bonded liquor from Canada. The bartender is on our payroll."

Cole tasted his drink and pronounced the whiskey authentic or a clever imitation.

"Am I correct in assuming that you gentlemen were participants in the late war," asked Cole.

"We both fought in France. Alexander with the Brits. The way things went, we count it our good fortune that the generals did not have us shooting at each other instead of the Krauts.

"I was bayoneted, shot, and left for dead by our illustrious enemy but here I sit drinking illegal liquids after being drug around a dance floor by a modern woman."

Cole noted with pleasure that he could say this freely to two men who shared his awe, that they were alive in such a new world, a place so removed from their lives before the war.

"My theory is that they took us all off to war and shot at us to toughen us up to face the prospect back home of no liquor and women with scanty clothes and the vote," said Bill.

Clover returned, makeup refreshed, and scowled at the men. Are you talking about the war?"

"Not at all, my dear. We are toasting the nineteenth amendment, Chin, Chin," replied Alexander, as he led the downing of another generous swig from their glasses.

While Clover still stood judgmentally over them, a callow young man approached her and asked her to favor him with a dance. She regarded him coolly and said," My intended prefers me to save all my dances for him," she gestured to Cole.

The young man said, "Pardon me, Sir, I do not mean to offend." He stumbled away with sufficient sway to suggest that a stint on the dance floor with him might have been hazardous to Clover's feet.

Bill asked, "Is Cole intended for ritual sacrifice or mummification? I know he is not your betrothed since he seems too intelligent a fellow to enlist for that."

Clover glared at Bill icily. "At least I have a gentleman with me tonight. You two never have young ladies with you, not even disreputable ones. I dare say that is understandable since all you do is drink and discuss the war, insurance, banks, and what the weather is doing to the crops," said Clover.

"Be fair, Clover, we are discussing how we make a living and our prospects. Men are the breadwinners. It is not easy for most of us. Your father has spoiled you all your life. You think money is just there for the taking and you like to be above the tedium and grubbiness of acquiring it. We do not have that luxury," replied Bill.

"Life is not just about earning a living. There is beauty, art, music, joy, wonder, and mystery. I want to live my life, really live it, not just exist, not just persevere,"

Clover heatedly enunciated the last of this proclamation. She downed another drink and pulled Cole back to the dance floor where she let the power of her anger energize her dance into a frenzy of motion.

Cole struggled to keep up but soon realized that Clover was only dimly aware of his presence. Her dance was not a partnership but a syncopated soliloquy, in which she screamed, *I am Clover and life has to deal with me on my terms.*

Cole tried to not look too awkward staying outside of her rapid-fire arms and legs undulated from one area of the dance floor to the next.

The band played a session of pounding jazz until abruptly they slipped into an old fashion waltz. Clover stood silently for several moments, her body still vibrating like a weed recovering from the last gust of wind from a cleansing storm.

Cole expected her to walk back to the table, but she finally looked up at him and seemed to really see him for the first time this evening. She smiled one of the most beautiful, radiant smiles Cole had ever seen, and nestled deeply into his arms for a gentle glide around the floor as the band played a familiar old tune.

As the song ended, Clover whispered, "Take me home."

Cole turned toward their table to say goodbye to Bill and Alexander, but Clover pulled him to the exit.

"Poor company will be with us always. Just wave goodbye," she said.

Cole waved at the two men across the room, gesturing at Clover and struggling as she pulled him to the door. The men laughed and waved, and suddenly Cole was outside in the cool night air with Clover holding him tight for warmth.

Back in the car, Cole retraced their journey from home and had gone about a mile when Clover ordered him to take a barely perceptible dirt path off the road, which ended up at a narrow tongue of water from a nearby lake.

Cole parked such that another car traversing the dirt

tract would not immediately see that another vehicle was already at the end of the course.

Clover took her shoes off and walked to the edge of the water. The inlet widened towards the lake, and Cole and Clover were treated to a vista of an erratic wind pushing waves about on the glittering moon-lit surface of the lake.

Cole thought Clover would be too cold to spend more than a few seconds out of the automobile, but she spent several minutes surveying the full moon and its playful illumination of the shifting ripples on the lake. An owl hooted nearby and the forest rustled around them with life.

Clover eventually took Cole's hand and led him back to the passenger door of his vehicle. She took his head in her hands and kissed him until he was running his hands over her body. Clover reached down and slipped her dress over her head.

As Cole suspected, she had nothing on underneath. Clover moved Cole's hand over her breasts and somehow managed to open the car door, pulling Cole onto the seat with her underneath him. The moonlight through the windshield made Clover's face glow and, in spite of the heat of his lust, Cole focused on the energy in her face as they made love.

Her face was never still, she was dreamy pleasure, teeth-clinched passion, alone in space and time, linked to him in a tightly gripped frenzy, eyes closed, eyes open and locked with his to infinity, and eyes open to the void.

She was all this and more, and Cole was connected to

another for the first time since Aurora had left his life. Eventually, they fell apart, spent and perspiring.

Cole retrieved Clover's dress and shoes and carefully brought the automobile back to the road. Clover curled up, with her feet underneath her, against the passenger door and said nothing to Cole on the way home.

He rubbed her leg and stroked her hair but she ignored him. She would not let him walk her to her door when they had reached her house.

As Cole tried to talk to her and kiss her, Clover put a hand on his lips gently and said, "No, please, do not care too much for me or expect anything from me, Cole. I am not for you, or anyone for that matter." She held his hand gently against her cheek, kissed it, and walked from the car to her door without looking back at the man who watched her with a pitiable aching loss in his heart.

Two days after his rendezvous with Clover, Cole made his way to Clover's front door soon after sunset and rang the bell. Catherine arrived and asked Cole in, but Cole demurred and asked if Clover was receiving visitors.

Catherine's smile faded, "I am sorry, Cole, she went out earlier. I do not know when she will return. May I tell her that you called? Won't you come in? I have not seen you in a while. We can catch up, and I have a new book I would like you to see."

"I apologize, Catherine, but I have work I need to

complete. I only interrupted it to talk with Clover for a minute. I will speak with her another time," said Cole.

Cole did return home but sat on his back porch sipping brandy and watching birds fluttering among the trees in his back yard.

Knowing that others could not see their playful antics in this light helped to lighten his melancholy a mite.

"Cole, are you back here?" Catherine stood at the edge of his porch unable to see where he sat.

"I am here, Catherine, let me turn on a light for you."

Catherine came up on the porch and sat by the chair where Cole had been ensconced. "How did you know I was here?" he asked.

"I saw you head this way, and there are not lights in the house," Catherine replied. "What are you doing out here in the dark?"

"Listening to the birds, sipping brandy. Would you care for a glass?" Cole asked.

"This is the pressing project you could not leave?" Catherine sniffed.

"I changed my mind. I decided the birds required my attention," answered Cole.

"I would think I ought to be even with the birds in eliciting your attention. Henceforth, I will wear feathers and tweet prettily," said Catherine.

"I am sorry. I really did change my mind about work and I am not pleasant company tonight," explained Cole.

"Well, I will suffer through that since I am going to

sit her with you for a while. You can even turn off the lights if you wish. I do not want to disturb your beaked buddies," Catherine said.

Cole laughed, "You are higher on my guest list than the birds. They make me smile. You make me laugh."

"I will settle for that. I will not take the risk of asking how I fit in compared to dogs and cats. Although, I will mention that I do not shed, and I never bite or scratch," Catherine said.

"There, we have it established, you are a truly superior guest and companion, and I am a cad for not accepting your invitation to visit with you earlier," said Cole with a chortle.

Catherine gazed at Cole for a while. "I know something happened between you and Clover, and she has hurt you. I know the look. I have seen it often enough. I do not speak for my sister and usually do not comment on her to anyone outside the family, but I am fond of you and I hate to see you sad. Clover is Clover. She is unique, strong-willed, and fiercely guards her independence. You cannot take perceived rejection by her too personally. She lives in a world that ignores the rules most of the rest of us live by."

"I understand, Catherine. A man does not have to have my training to fathom Clover's personality, but she is fun and personable, and even a man like me can be forgiven for hoping to be that elusive missing puzzle piece that will augment her personality and convince her to consider creating a new life as a couple," said Cole.

"You left ravishingly beautiful out of the fun and personable description," corrected Catherine.

Cole laughed, "Alright, I admit it, Catherine, a fun and personable plain Jane might not have commanded my attention."

Cole abruptly leaned forward in his chair.

"Well, Detective Ross, this is a special evening for me, first an unexpected visit from my lovely neighbor and now an even more unexpected visit from you," called Cole. "Step up on the porch and join us."

Ross came up the stairs, obviously a little flustered by Catherine's presence. Cole stood, shook the detective's hand, and introduced Ross to Catherine.

"I know your father, Miss, and I have seen you and your sister from a distance on many occasions. Your father is fortunate to have such beautiful daughters," Detective Ross said.

"Thank you, Detective, and I am indeed my father's daughter. I know my presence is interfering with the discussion of your business with Dr. Sterling. I will retreat to my house. Good evening to both of you," she replied.

Detective Ross blushed, "I apologize, Miss Catherine, I did not intend to disturb your visit."

"Think nothing of it, Detective. I have plenty of time to set Dr. Sterling on the right course. A women's work is never done," Catherine said.

"I do apologize, Doctor. I did not mean to disturb your evening." He glanced at Catherine as she walked back to her house. "She is a lovely young woman." Detective Ross observed.

"And fun and personable," said Cole.

"Oh?"

"A private joke between Catherine and myself. What can I do for you?" asked Cole as he gestured at a chair for Detective Ross.

"We have an unusual situation in the city. An odd crime probably connected to unexplained disappearances over the last month. A few days ago, a patrol car happened upon a stalled truck at the edge of town. No one was with the truck, and the officer looked into the back and saw fingers just sticking out from under a pile of potato sacks. A women's body was under the pile covered by a canvas sheet. The potatoes had shifted with the truck's movement, and the body had moved enough under the canvas to allow the tips of the fingers to be seen. The officer felt the block which was still warm. He made sure the truck could not be started and searched the immediate area but found no one. He summoned help, and we extended our search, but nothing useful was located.

"The body was that of a prostitute who was last seen a day earlier. She had not been working. She was with her monthly and her roommate, another prostitute, thought she might have gone to see her mother. The girl had not been gone long enough to worry her friend," Ross paused in his exposition. "No doubt you wonder why I am telling you this, Dr. Sterling."

Cole interrupted, "Call me Cole."

"There are two reasons, Cole, for one you are unusually insightful, that I know from personal experience." The detective paused again but did not elaborate, knowing that Cole understood him. "The second reason is that we have suspects and, it turns out, these suspects have been asking around about you."

Cole had been agitated by Detective Ross's appearance but had been relieved up to now by the subject of his monologue. The heavy weight in his stomach returned.

"Have you taken these people into custody? Do you know why they are interested in me? And you said, 'disappearances,'" Cole interjected.

"Several women have gone missing. Prostitutes and party girls, inhabitants of the sleazy world of speakeasies. The three men of interest to the police are new arrivals to these parts and were seen with at least some of the women. I have not spoken with the men and have no grounds to arrest them. My informants are clear that they had specifically asked about your activities and location. Their motivation for interest in you is unknown."

"What are their names?" asked Cole.

"David Frame, Frank Bowling, who says he is a factotum for the third man, who claims he is a nobleman from Germany. Baron Gerbold."

Cole sat up in his chair. "I met Gerbold in Brussels. He was with the men I believe killed the woman that I had hoped to marry. No one ever was prosecuted for her death. Frame is a blight on the earth. He practices something he calls practical magic and has written luridly about drug addiction. He revels in selfishness and moral degeneracy. He is notorious for his views and practices and has an unsavory following that attends his lectures and buy his books. He relishes being labeled as evil."

Cole delivered his assessment to Ross with an icy passion that surprised Ross.

"I see I have come to the right person for help. Were Frame and Bowling in Brussels also?"

"I believe I met Bowling briefly. I know of Frame because the murder inquiry found him to be a close associate of the presumed killer. Frame, of course, denied any connection or knowledge of the murder. That may be true, but his despicable philosophy may have played a role in pushing a mentally ill man to harm the woman I loved. I am repulsed by everything that Frame stands for." Cole forced himself to reduce the heat of his comments.

He acknowledged to himself the hypocrisy of a murderous blood drinker condemning a man who may, at most, have only degraded the vulnerable, not actually inflicted significant physical injury.

Nonetheless, Cole knew to the depth of his being that a man who gleefully rejected good and embraced evil was capable of anything that would not surely land him in prison or standing at the gallows.

"Will you go with me to pay a visit on these fellows? The reason for wanting to see you may be pertinent to my investigation, and I would like your impression of their responses to my questions?" asked Ross.

"Certainly," said Cole. "I have a few questions myself."

"Could you go with me tonight? I ought to see them right away. I apologize for the timing, but this is a murder investigation after all," Ross explained.

Cole plucked his jacket from a peg by the door. He

walked into the cool evening air, along with Ross, with a foreboding that once again his life might be changing forever and again completely out of his control.

Ross drove Cole to what appeared to be a grand house only a few blocks from the main business section of town. There were no lights on the front of the house and they entered by a side door discretely illuminated.

The doorman was pleasant, recognized Ross and allowed them access to a handsome elliptical room, which opened out in three directions to larger rooms replete with well-dressed men and women, who were conversing or eating at café tables, or in one of the rooms playing roulette or dealer-supervised card games.

In the game room, Ross approached an elegant dark-haired man at a small, but impressive, mahogany bar.

"I am surprised to see you, Detective, knowing how you feel about my club," the man said.

"I am here on business, Mr. Holiday. May I introduce Dr. Sterling? He is kindly assisting me," replied Ross.

"Welcome to my private club, Dr. Sterling. If you are interested in membership, I will happily accommodate you. Unfortunately, Detective Ross and I differ in interpretation of the new law regarding the rights of private clubs. I take solace in the fact that his superiors see things my way," Holiday said unctuously.

Cole could tell Ross was struggling to control himself. "There are three men who are frequent visitors to your establishment, Mr. Holiday. I need to interview them regarding a serious crime. Their names are Frame, Bowling, and Gerbold."

Holiday arched his eyebrows. "These are respectable

men, Detective Ross, and my club is a sanctuary. Your supervisors would not appreciate a scene here that might embarrass any number of my important guests."

"I will not disturb your visitors. I just need a few minutes with these men to establish some basic facts," Ross countered.

Holiday started to protest but stopped and smiled. "I believe you will find them upstairs. You know the way."

Cole was surprised at Holiday's sudden cooperation. Ross, however, immediately made his way up to the second floor, where men were drinking and conversing at tables, with a scattering of minimally-dressed young women in their midst.

Ross, apparently, had descriptions that lead him directly to the table of the men he sought. They were alone and were quietly conversing.

Ross introduced himself and invited himself to sit with them. He ignored Cole, who stood silently.

"You gentlemen appear to be among the last to see a young woman recently murdered, Virginia Sweet. Can you tell me about your last encounter?" asked Ross.

The Baron smirked, "My companions and I are bon vivants and connoisseurs of pretty women. To narrow the relationship possibilities, was she a lady for hire?"

Ross was clearly irritated by the Baron but replied, "Virginia was a prostitute, and I understand she was a favorite of yours in this establishment."

"We certainly know a Virginia but never got to know her last name. We have not seen her in a few days. Just this evening, we inquired about her. No one mentioned her coming to an untimely end. We will miss her, but I do not see how we can help you. We never saw her except in this house. But I must interrupt; you have an old friend of mine with you? A pleasure to see you, Dr. Sterling. I heard about your loss shortly after my party left Belgium. You know my constant companion, Mr. Bowling, but you have not met the noted author David Frame." The Baron replied.

Cole stoically shook the men's hands but refused to sit. "Can you tell me anything about your friend, Cartan? The police identified him as Aurora's killer, but he has completely disappeared," asked Cole.

"He left our companionship just before we left for Paris. He said nothing to explain his divergence from the planned excursion. He simply was gone," replied the Baron.

"Why were you looking for Dr. Sterling, Baron?" asked Ross.

"We had heard he had ended up in this rustic, if you will excuse me, provincial place, and merely wished to give him our regards as we traveled through to Hot Springs," replied the Baron.

"This is a curious itinerary to Hot Springs," stated Ross.

"We came down from Washington, where we had a little business and decided to take a more scenic train ride," the Baron explained.

Mr. Holiday was beckoning to Ross from a discrete distance. Ross excused himself and spoke briefly to Holiday before returning with a clinched jaw and flushed face.

In the short interval of his absence, Frame spoke

with a lurid grim, "You know those girls will let you make discrete slices on their inner thighs, where you can savor the warm trickle of blood while you enjoy their usual attractions. Of course, you have to prepare them properly with the right amount of cocaine up the nose. The experience is really very sensual. I recommend it to you. You look a little wan."

Cole was fighting mad and wanted to tear Frame's throat out. Ross grasped his shoulders firmly. Ross had not heard Frame, but on his return, instantly saw that Cole was about to lose all control.

"Come on, we have to leave immediately," Ross commanded.

Ross handed the Baron his card. "Call or write me if you remember anything useful about Virginia."

Cole followed Ross out with great personal restraint. He knew these men had killed the hapless Virginia, and he knew they probably knew where Cartan was and why Aurora had been killed. He would have to seek them out, but this was not the place.

Outside Ross said, "I knew Holiday gave in quickly just to bolt to the telephone and call his protectors. We had a couple of minutes at best to meet the Baron and his buddies before we were officially told to leave the premises."

Back in his car, Ross continued, "What did Frame say to you to cause you to look like you were about to throttle him?"

"It is complicated. Frame is a bottom dweller, and he implied that I was a member of his club by confiding a detail of his sick deviancy as if I were a fellow traveler."

"But you won't tell me exactly what he said?" asked Ross.

"I told you it is complicated. I cannot discuss it here," snapped Cole.

"Do you think they killed Virginia?"

"Absolutely, but they said nothing just now that implicated them. They are wicked but intelligent and sly. They are not going to carelessly expose themselves," replied Cole.

"Why would they kill the girl?" Ross asked.

"Was the corpse mutilated?" Cole asked abruptly.

Ross looked at him warily. "She had cuts on her legs but they were a few days old and of no real significance. She died from being bled out by a sharp cut on her neck, while apparently suspended by her ankles. Similar to draining the blood from a pig."

Cole was quiet for a minute. "I want a warm cup of coffee. Is there a quiet place we could talk? I am putting my confidence in you, Detective. I cannot help you without doing that. You will hear things you will find difficult to believe, and my continued well-being will be vulnerable to your good will."

Ross was silent until they pulled up at a small café, where he was apparently a regular, based on the warm greeting from the squat, swarthy man behind the counter.

Only a few patrons were still around this late in the evening, and they were all up front talking to the owner.

The establishment offered a single row of stools except for a lonely booth in back by the toilet. Ross and Cole secured coffee and sat there well out of ear range of the others.

"I will relate this succinctly. Your credulity may be less tried if you hear this simply without elaboration. I was an Army surgeon in the war. My field hospital was overrun, and I sustained mortal wounds. Beyond any doubt, I should have died in France, and I would have except for the fortuitous intervention of a wealthy Frenchwoman who used her estate and resources to care for allied soldiers mentally traumatized by battle.

Because of her home's proximity to where I was injured, I was brought to her home for assistance and, in my case, to offer me comfort in my final hours. The lady in question, who I came to know and love, was named Aurora, and for reasons she could never adequately explain, gave me a primitive transfusion of her blood. I needed blood but what she provided would have been inadequate and risky for me to receive.

"Aurora gave me this gift because she knew that her blood conferred amazing restorative properties. She also knew that the benefits were, in many ways, outweighed by unalterable life changing loss of everyday human capabilities.

"I hide from the sun. My flesh practically sizzles and my eyes would scorch with unfiltered exposure to sunlight. Food is no longer of interest, and I eat minimally. The truly disturbing feature of my transformation is that I must have blood to survive.

"Aurora knew when she saved my life that she was

condemning me to this shadowy world, which would be repulsive to my former friends and family. She had lived for decades within the confines of this new existence and knew that there was more curse than blessing to her act of salvation."

"What do you mean you must have blood to live," Ross inquired.

"I drink it like you would a glass of beer. I only have animal blood in this city, but Aurora had paid a donor and we drank human blood, which is both incomparably satisfying and surprisingly nutritious. My stamina and senses are dulled by the absence of human blood," Cole replied.

Ross stared at Cole, his face a fluid amalgam of suspicion, incredulity, and contempt.

Before Ross could interject, Cole continued, "I am not a mythical vampire. I am mortal. My heart beats. I believe I have a soul. Except for the differences I have related, my needs are similar to yours. The Baron is like me, as was the man who killed Aurora.

"The Baron manipulates Frame, implying he will convert him, but he has a price that is currently unmet. I have no idea what the Baron wants, why he and Frame are here, nor the basis for their interest in me. Had I been alone with them in a nonpublic place, I would have sought the answer to everything I want to know, even if I had to maim them."

"You may have a soul, Cole, but it is not peaceful, reverent, or patient," Detective Ross pronounced solemnly.

"I suspect you understand that condition quite well," replied Cole.

"Indeed, I do," Ross replied with a sad, weak smile. "But you will forgive me if I view you now with some suspicion. How can I know you are not part of this? After all, you would have relished sipping Virginia's blood if it were at your table."

"I would have gladly offered the lady a nice sum for a pint of her best, but I would not have injured her to obtain it. Because I do believe I have a soul to protect. I avoid intentionally injuring the innocent. Virginia may not have been part of respectable society, but speaking theoretically, I have no reason to assume she had ever seriously harmed anyone," Cole said.

Detective Ross stared glumly at Cole for a while. "You do realize this is a preposterous situation. I will suspend disbelief for now and accept your version of events, but if you become implicated, or if I realize you are attempting to make a fool of me, I will grind you down to powder."

"I, by divulging my condition to you, have already put my life in your hands. Even rumors of my true nature would destroy my career," stated Cole quietly.

Ross shrugged, "So how do I convict these men?"

Cole replied, "With your usual police work. They are clever, but they might have been too confident. Someone may have seen something. Investigate them closely."

Ross said, "They will know and may leave town."

"They were here for a reason. I will visit the Baron at his hotel. Maybe I can get something out of him that will help both of us. Knowing their true purpose may reveal weaknesses we can exploit," said Cole.

"You understand you may be in danger. Their goal may be to kill you like your friend. Apparently, you do not know why she was murdered," said Ross.

"If the Baron tells me anything about Aurora's death, the risk to me will be worthwhile. I am compelled to know why she died. I will take my chances."

Ross stood up wearily from the booth. "Come on, I will take you home."

Cole said, "You know, Detective, I told you to call me Cole, but you never said what I should call you other than detective."

"Everyone just calls me Ross."

"You don't have a first name?" asked Cole.

"Millard. Like I said, call me Ross."

In the days that followed, Cole weighed his new circumstances and was troubled in heart and mind. He had given Ross power over the entire course of his life, and Clover had pierced his heart, leaving him her emotional captive. He longed to see her, but she came home late almost every night with one of her gentleman friends. He watched her walk into her home and ritually look up at his darkened windows as if she sensed his presence and heartbreak. He was too proud to attempt to see her again, at least for now.

Cole called on the Baron at his hotel but had to leave a message for him asking to meet him privately in his suite. His note suggested a specific time and provided his telephone number.

The Baron never called, but Cole went to the Baron's room at the time he had specified. To Cole's relief, the Baron opened his door and invited him in with a grand flourish. They appeared to be alone.

"I appreciate your receiving me, Baron. I was unsuccessful in locating you while I was in Europe. After your initial statement to the police, no one seemed to be aware of your whereabouts," Cole said flatly.

The Baron offered Cole brandy, which he declined. "I am rather a peripatetic type, Dr. Sterling, and I have many friends across Europe. I follow my whims. My business affairs are well managed. I have the good fortune to be able to indulge myself and wander as I please. I apologize that my absence caused you additional discomfort after Aurora's death. She was a magnificent lady."

"I will come directly to the point, Baron. Do you believe Marie-Henri killed Aurora, and if so, why?" asked Cole.

The Baron picked up a glowing cigar from an ashtray on a side table and twirled it between his thumb and middle finger before reverently inhaling a fragrant column of smoke.

He exhaled slowly and completely before answering. "I do not know, Dr. Sterling. I think it is possible. Marie-Henri was very agitated after encountering Aurora. He still viewed her as his wife. Seeing her with another man was infuriating to him.

"On the evening we crossed paths, he had drunk

with abandon, even for him. After seeing the two of you, he impugned your morals and made a wild assortment of threats. My comrades and I tried to dissuade him from seeking you out, but he left right after you did. I had hopes to refocus his thoughts to a concern of mine and would have suggested that we contact Aurora the following day to discuss my request. I had my own selfish interests, but thought another meeting with her might allow him to begin to accept that she was no longer part of his life.

"Unfortunately, as I said, he stormed out of the restaurant and my comrades and I never saw him again. Perhaps, he actually intended to do you harm but encountered her and, in his drunken state, could not contain himself. Mere speculation, conjecture of course, but plausible."

"What did you want from Aurora?" asked Cole pointedly.

"As you know, there are very few like us in the world and avoidance of the sun is a heavy burden for all of us. Individually, we have unusual strengths, gifts really. It had occurred to me that partaking of the blood of another of our kind might further enhance our capabilities. Perhaps, even to the point of surmounting our sensitivity to sunlight. Having the blood of another similar being, but one not related to us, that is, not our transformer, might offer surprising enrichment and transformation."

"Surely, you have already attempted this experiment with Marie-Henri and perhaps another," said Cole.

"Indeed, I have. The blood is invigorating but the

effect is not long lasting nor substantive," replied the Baron.

"Marie-Henri was, in a manner of speaking, of Aurora's lineage. If his blood was not particularly useful, why ask for some of Aurora's?" asked Cole.

"An appropriate question. I suspect Aurora was more powerful than Marie-Henri and everyone else for that matter. For one thing, there are rumors her grandfather was much more powerful than any of us about today. There are even rumors that when he wanted he could endure sunlight for a period of time.

"Aurora's blood derived directly from this prototypical source and reasonably might have great potency. Of course, this is all speculative now with her passing. "This brings me now to why I sought you out. Your blood derives from Aurora and perhaps, because of the peculiarities of your constitution, your blood is more characteristic of her grandfather's than was Marie-Henri's. I hoped to persuade you to allow me to withdraw an aliquot for my testing," the Baron explained.

The thought of giving this man with the soulless eyes some of his blood was chilling and repulsive to Cole. The Baron proposed a persuasive scenario, implicating a lone deranged man in Aurora's death, but Cole's intuition suggested that the Baron was more involved in her murder than he admitted.

The longer the Baron spoke, the more Cole was convinced that the Baron had hoped to force Aurora to relinquish some of her blood, or perhaps had wanted Marie-Henri to abduct her so that she could become a source of his own private, magnificent elixir.

Cole could readily envision Aurora forcefully resisting Marie-Henri, either acting alone or with others, with a resulting violent conclusion. The Baron's exposition was rational, his manner respectful and solicitous, but Cole felt confident that the Baron had a hand in her death, even if he was not the proximate cause.

Cole wanted from the depth of his being to dispatch the Baron on this very spot, but Cole knew he could not escape the consequences of killing the Baron as long as police attention was concentrated on him. Cole would have to wait for the opportunity for the Baron to experience the administration of Cole's justice, and there were many questions he would answer truthfully before his last breath. Cole could restrain himself only by silently vowing that the Baron would pay completely for Aurora's murder in due time.

Cole stood and thanked the Baron for his time.

"Do you have any idea where I might find Marie-Henri?" he asked.

"None whatsoever, my dear fellow," the Baron replied.

Cole forced himself to shake the Baron's hand and said, "I will consider your request to assist your experimentation. Discussion of Aurora's death has disturbed me too much to properly consider your project at present."

Cole exited the Baron's suite quickly. He hoped the Baron would attribute his sudden departure to Cole's stated emotional distress. Fortunately, Cole was convinced the Baron did not have Cole's intuition capacity and did not detect Cole's fiery murderous resolve to bring him down.

The next days were trying for Cole. He ruminated incessantly about the Baron, Aurora, and Clover. Cole shared his thoughts with Ross but could not provide Ross with anything to use against the Baron and his friends.

Frustrated by his powerlessness, he paced around his home and attended to his patients perfunctorily, barely suppressing his internal rage and frustration. It was in this agitated state that Cole received the news of Clover's mysterious departure.

Catherine came to his home to tell him that Clover had not come home the previous night and had telephoned that morning to say that she was on her way to Charleston with her new friends. Clover had not sounded her usual self and had left without any of her clothes. She was vague and mysterious, claiming she was with friends of Dr. Sterling, a Baron Gerbold and a famous writer named Frame.

Catherine was crying and said she knew her sister was unconventional and flaunted propriety, but she had never done anything like this.

Her parents were about to call the police but wanted Catherine to ask Cole if he understood any of this. Cole was concerned for Clover but felt oddly subdued and focused by this development.

The Baron had examined Cole's life and had fired a shot over Cole's bow using the only weapon he could find, Clover. The Baron wanted Cole's cooperation and was determined to compel it.

"Go back home, Catherine. Tell your parents I will contact Detective Ross. He is already interested in these men for other reasons. I will leave immediately for Charleston and Ross will probably go with me. I do know the Baron and Frame. They are not friends of mine, but I doubt they will harm Clover," said Cole.

Cole did not have the heart to tell Catherine that the men were his enemies and that Clover was being used as a pawn by men who would not hesitate to injure Clover if it served their selfish purposes.

"Dad telephoned Alexander Forester and Bill Pine. He knows they often see Clover and in their own way, try to be protective of her. They asked him to have you call them," said Catherine. "They want to help if they can."

Cole accepted a note with telephone numbers and escorted Catherine to the door. She hugged him tightly for several seconds and kissed him on the cheek before walking away.

Cole telephoned Ross first and got him to agree to the trip. Ross muttered something about not having any jurisdiction but wanted these bastards any way he could get them.

In due course, the four men agreed to set out at nightfall by automobile. Alexander volunteered the use of one of his automobiles, and they loaded up at Cole's house. Ross sniffed at the duffel bags in the luggage compartment, commenting, "You boys appear well prepared for disagreeable men or ornery elephants. I am glad I am on your side."

Cole sat in the back with Ross. He waited until they were well started before telling Alexander and Bill about his intolerance to sunlight, explaining that with dawn he would have to cover up completely.

Cole told them about the source of his affliction but did not mention his need for blood. He hoped that there would not be a need to disclose his shame and his weakness to them. The two friends laughed about crossing Cole off the list for their summer beach excursion, but appeared to politely accept the validity of his claim.

Cole was grateful for their tolerance but suspected that they silently believed Cole to be yet another neurasthenic war veteran who had substituted the compulsion to hide from the sun for fainting spells, limb weakness, or twitching.

The ride from Knoxville to Charleston was slow and at times challenging. The men wiled away the time by conversing about the best way to find the Baron in Charleston and a plethora of other topics from deer hunting to how bankers and tobacco farmers depended on each other.

They collectively acknowledged that the Baron may not have taken Clover to Charleston at all, but they spent little time on this possibility since the rational extension of this line of thought made their mission quixotic and Clover's survival unlikely.

At dawn, they drove into Charleston with Cole covered from head to toe. Bill had laughed after Ross had helped Cole with his garb. "I am driving into

Charleston this fine morning with H. G. Wells' invisible man. I guess it could be worse. I could be traveling with Bram Stokers' Dracula," Ross looked over at Cole and smirked.

They stopped at a hotel near the Embarcadero that Alexander had frequented in recent years. They registered with minimal fuss and genteel inattention to Cole's odd dress.

Alexander convinced the concierge to call a number of the better hotels in Charleston to ascertain if the Baron and company had set up court in any of their establishments. When this effort failed, he suggested that they all get some rest and start after sundown making the rounds of the local speakeasies. Cole was frustrated that they might be near Clover but unable to rescue her. He was about to protest when Ross spoke up.

"There is still work to be done in the day. The Baron might have selected a lesser hotel without a telephone. I will look into that possibility and will pay a courtesy call on the local police. Even though I am here to locate Clover, I am also here to look for murder suspects. I may not have official status, but the local police do not want possible murderers and abductors in their town. They will help me find the Baron and Clover."

"Bill and Alexander, you should sleep a couple of hours and then when I return we will split up to call on all the addresses I have identified. If we do not have any luck today, then we will have to investigate the local watering holes tonight. This is like most police work, a lot of shoe leather is expended.

"Cole, I know you do not want to hear this, but you

have to stay in your room. Your roaming around in your current outfit will attract attention we cannot afford. Some folks that we need to interrogate will not talk around you, and the Baron will hear of your presence within hours. The Baron knows we will be looking, but we might surprise him with our alacrity. If I uncover anything promising, I assure you I will call your room right away," Ross said.

Cole wanted to protest but knew Ross was correct. He had felt powerless before, but now he was overwhelmed by a wave of melancholy. If Clover died or was severely injured, Cole could not fathom how he would survive the blow to his psyche. He silently went to his room and, after securing the curtains, lay in bed on his back and watched the slow hypnotic gyrations of the blades of the ceiling fan.

Cole was startled awake by the telephone on the side table, surprised that he had fallen asleep so readily. He tried to clear the sleep from his voice as he answered.

Ross wearily recounted his progress. "I talked to police, hotels, and assorted low lifes, but only made headway by following up on a tip from a local detective. He suggested I check with a couple of small boat shippers who routinely run visitors over to one of the barrier islands where a high-class den of iniquity operates. This place is expensive and caters to well-healed patrons, who are looking for more than illegal alcohol to satisfy their exotic sinful tastes.

"The detective has no direct experience but has reliable reports that this off-shore enterprise, called The Haven, has wicked entertainment for the flesh to rival an ancient Babylonian brothel. My new friend has no jurisdiction there but would love having some details to provide to those who can rightfully claim oversight. He is disturbed that there are even rumors of people going out on the island and not returning.

"After pursuing obvious contacts, I went down to the dock and found a captain who told me that a party that fit my description had gone over early evening yesterday with one of his competitors. Unfortunately, that skipper was not there but will probably be back around sundown. I intend to get a little sleep and we can go over at sunset to interview this new contact. If he confirms the sighting, we will work out passage to The Haven to see if Clover and the Baron are truly there," Ross reported.

Cole hung up the telephone and got up slowly from the bed. He still felt drained. His reflection in an expensive, decorative wall mirror revealed a haggard, thin, pale man with dark circles under his eyes. This man clearly needed nourishment.

After calling room service to request a bucket of chipped or shaved ice, Cole rummaged in his valise for one of the sealed containers he had prepared for this contingency. At home, Cole had been experimenting with methods to store blood without refrigeration for use on trips or with unexpected supply interruptions.

His efforts were desultory and in their early stages. He had not anticipated having to utilize a primitive experiment to sustain himself at this point in time.

Cole examined the sealed can he removed from a padded leather pouch. The sterilized can had been carefully filled with bull's blood with traces of chemical preservatives and anticoagulants. A stopcock on the can had enabled residual air to be removed with a vacuum pump.

After slowly opening the stop cork to the room air, Cole punctured the can and poured the contents into a table glass. He smelled the liquid with the air of a connoisseur of fine wine and then cautiously sipped it. He was relieved that the blood appeared potable and possessed minimally disagreeable aftertaste.

While nothing surpassed the invigorating taste of fresh, warm human blood, even high-quality animal blood sometimes was better drunk cool or iced. This particular specimen required icing.

Cole covered the glass with a handkerchief and waited impatiently for the bellboy to arrive. He tipped the old man who delivered the ice at the door. The man had intended to bring the ice bucket into the room, but his curiosity vanished with the sizable tip Cole placed in his hand.

Illegal spirits and wild women were fine by him as long as the patrons had the good sense to pay an appropriate luxury tax to their ever-handy bellman.

The ice was stirred into the blood and impatiently drank while merely cool. Within seconds of draining the contents of the glass, Cole felt flushed and invigorated. The man in the mirror was no longer pale and the dark circles at the eyes were barely noticeable. Cole opened a second can, and this time allowed the ice to properly chill the contents of the glass. He drank the fluid slowly and savored the complex flavors of the concoction.

The chemicals still were off-putting but the overall effect was similar to drinking cheap wine when you desperately needed a drink. The liquid quenched his hunger and the taste met his needs at that moment in time.

Cole stripped and washed in a basin before dressing in fresh clothing from his vehicle. A new man now occupied the mirror, a fresh, youngish, virile specimen up to any task that fate placed in his path.

With the day fading fast, Cole left his lair and took the stairs to the lobby to meet the other warriors in his makeshift band. Stepping into the hotel bar jauntily, Cole met a barrage of loud banter from Bill and Alexander.

"Look at him. He is not only alive, he is positively bouncy. I have never seen a man recuperate so well from a mere nap. Come over here, you have a great selection at your disposal, root beer, sarsaparilla, or Coca-Cola? You can even get coffee," said Bill.

Alexander leaned over and whispered in Cole's ear, "Our barman can discreetly sweeten your choice for a well-deserved tip."

"Actually, I will have a root beer. That should suit me fine right now," said Cole.

Detective Ross walked into the room, gloomy and disheveled.

"Did you get any rest, Detective?" asked Cole.

"I barely closed my eyes." He scowled at the barman and asked for black coffee. "As soon as I down this, we should try to locate our boat captain. I am afraid someone will engage him before we can talk to him," Ross said irritably.

Cole surmised that, beyond his fatigue, Ross was frustrated by the lack of his usual helpers and by all the restraints tying his hands in pursuing this investigation his way. Ross had up to now provided the bulk of the labor for this search. Cole could understand his testiness.

Cole waited silently for Ross to drink his coffee while Alexander and Bill chattered quietly about a private party they were anticipating back home.

Ross did seem nearly his usual self after his beverage, and the men set out for the dock in the pleasant early evening, a gentle breeze rustling their hair as they strolled.

Ross spied his prey from afar and strode purposefully to an old but well-kept wooden fishing boat at the spot where Ross had been told the boat he sought would be tied up. A deeply tanned, weather-worn man in his fifties was inspecting the dock fittings when they came alongside.

"Ahoy, Captain, may we have a few minutes of your time?" called Ross.

"What might you need?" responded the Captain warily.

"I understand you ran a party over to The Haven yesterday. We want to verify if they are a group we are seeking."

"My parties are private, whether they fish or don't. I stay out of their affairs. They stay out of mine," the Captain replied.

"I admire your professionalism, Captain, but the men we want have abducted a young woman. This is her photograph, and this is a shot taken from a distance of the three men." Ross handed the photograph over the railing to the Captain who took them sullenly from his hand.

Cole was surprised Ross had these photographs and again shuddered with paranoiac realization at the formidable foe Ross would be if he were attempting to construct a case against Cole.

"Is this woman your daughter?" asked the Captain.

"She is these gentlemen's friend and her father asked us to bring her safely home. The men with her are not respectable sorts and are suspected of doing harm to many young women."

"Her father hired you?" queried the Captain. The satchels and canvas bags sitting on the planks of the dock had not escaped his attention.

"We are friends of the family only, not hired bounty hunters," replied Ross.

"But hunters you are nonetheless," countered the Captain. He had no intention of being taken for a fool. "The men were here, as you say, but they had three women with them, not one. The girl in the photograph was one of the three."

The four men looked at each other uneasily as they pondered this new development. Into the silence left by their bewilderment, the Captain interjected, "The girl you want seemed to be with a friend; the third woman was older and worn around the edges. What my wife would call a floozy."

Alexander stepped forward and spoke to the Captain. "I have $300 to pay for our passage out to The Haven to land us discretely and to wait for us. On our return, you get another $300," said Alexander. He opened his right hand to reveal a roll of large bank notes.

"We have to leave now and be back no later than sunrise," replied the Captain.

"We should get underway then," said Ross.

"Welcome aboard, Gentlemen. I'll cast off immediately. Another group is to be here soon for a little fishing. I would like to spare myself the embarrassment of having them curse at me as we head out."

The four men quickly scurried aboard and introduced themselves by their first names only. The Captain pocketed his $300, making note that Alexander did indeed have the money for their return passages.

As the Captain hustled off to expedite their departure, he announced with a smile, "I am the one and only Captain Abraham, Gentlemen, and I will indeed keep my end of the bargain, you can rest easy on that."

Captain Abraham readied his vessel and pulled away from the dock with surprising alacrity. The four men set up the folding chairs the captain had gestured at, but found the motion of the boat too wild to allow them to sit.

The chairs would be unusable except when the boat was at rest or possibly at a slow cruising speed. The group leaned against the worn railing while the boat pitched from side to side as Captain Abraham pushed the old boat harshly through the choppy water at top speed.

With the exception of Cole, the passengers struggled hard with sea sickness and watched fixedly in the bright moonlight their rapidly approaching destination across the water, hoping to avoid regurgitation. When near the island, the Captain swung the boat about sharply and began to parallel the shore. He reduced his speed significantly, which gave his passengers hope that they would survive their voyage without embarrassing themselves.

The boat arced along the shoreline to the back of the island out of sight of the mainland. The Captain gave wide birth to a well-kept pier that appeared to be the point of embarkation for The Haven. The boat continued around to an akilter, battered pier in a small cove away from the main pier.

Captain Abraham cautiously pulled alongside the decrepit structure and tied up at a remaining pier post that looked sound.

"I know it is about ready to fall in, but if you pick your steps carefully you can make it to the shore. There is an overgrown but passable path to The Haven. Once you are away, I will anchor offshore a ways and do a little fishing for appearances," said Captain Abraham.

Alexander and Bill pulled several battery-powered hand torches from their bags.

"You boys really are boy scouts, aren't you," said Ross.

"Where do you think we learned to smoke and drink?" replied Bill.

The group slowly picked their way across the creaking boards of the fragile pier illuminating each step with their hand torches and carefully spacing themselves so as not to overload a particular section of the rotting structure.

Lush vegetation surrounded the termination of the pier and lead directly onto a nearly erased ,narrow dirt path. The men stopped at the edge of the path and gave a final wave to Captain Abraham, who set out for deeper water at their signal. With the Captain's gaze directed to his labor, Alexander and Bill found pistols in their bags that fit handily in their coat pockets.

"The Captain cannot testify to items he never saw," noted Bill.

"I definitely need to keep a closer eye on you boys back in Knoxville," said Ross. "By the way," he continued, "If I am ever kidnapped, I elect Alexander to pay my ransom. You have no trouble dispensing copious amounts of cash out of your pockets at just the right time. For what you paid our good Captain, I would have pulled you over on a raft swimming with the tow rope between my teeth."

"I am the Wainwright family banker. I have carte blanche to pay necessary expenses to ensure Clover's return, but I assure you, Detective Ross, if you are kidnapped, I will make a sizable contribution to your ransom fund. I could not bear the thought of you locked in villainous clutches," Alexander replied.

All the men laughed as they began to troop along the dark path that was sporadically merging with the surrounding woods. Their progress was slowed by frequent consultations about the way the path had veered.

Soon they saw lights in the distance and heard the pulsing beat of a jazz band. As they crept closer to The Haven, they realized that the music originated from a live band not phonographic records. The path stopped at a bushy overgrowth just short of the lawn surrounding The Haven.

The proprietors of The Haven did not want the entrance to the trail to be evident while standing on the cleared area around the main building. This structure was an older two story house that had been carefully repaired and repainted. There were a few outbuildings, one which housed a generator to supply electricity for the interior lighting, and some well-positioned outside lights that illuminated the rough lawn that was the best that the island soil and weather permitted.

No one was walking on the lawn nearest the men as they worked their way off the trail. They expected to see people sitting on the screened veranda, but it was also bare. The four men looked briefly at each other and walked slowly to the steps that brought them to the veranda and front door. The veranda screen door was unlatched and the front door was open.

The Haven seemed to be comfortable with the security provided by their isolation. The four men walked into an atrium with closed doors to the right and left and a wide hallway directly ahead. Laughter, music and a beery smell emanated from down the hallway. There they found an expansive room with an old-fashioned saloon bar against the wall immediately to their right.

Several small tables were scattered around the room, all populated with laughing inebriated people. A small dance floor was the center of attention for the gathering.

A single couple occupied the parquet. An older red-faced man with a well-developed paunch clumped around the square attempting to grasp a young brunette woman shimmying seductively in a bright yellow dress. One strap of her dress had fallen off her shoulder exposing most of her right breast. The club patrons were laughing to the point of tears.

"That's right, Judge, get her to Fox Trot right with your hand on her ass," called out a nearby spectator.

"You'll catch her, Judge, she can't keep it up forever," hollered another man.

The cat calls and raucous laughter continued while the four men approached the bar and signaled a bartender. They were approached by a neatly-dressed young man trying to suppress the laughter he had been sharing with the assembly.

"What can I do for you gents," asked the bartender.

"We are looking for friends of ours. Three men, came over last night with two women. One of the men is Baron Gerbold," said Ross over the music and laughter.

"They are upstairs. I have not seen them down here. I sent up some drinks earlier," replied the bartender.

"Which room?" asked Ross.

The bartender had stopped laughing and carefully appraised the four men.

"We do not let visitors announce themselves to our guests. Are you gentlemen here for the evening or will you be staying overnight?" the bartender inquired.

"We are just here to party with our friends," said Ross.

Alexander placed a fold of large bills onto the bar near the bartender's hand. The young man glanced at the currency before saying, "I will need to have our manager assist you. I will summon him immediately. Please make yourselves comfortable."

Alexander pocketed the scorned cash as the bartender went out a door at the end of the bar. He said to his friends, "I will remain in place. You all go upstairs and find them. Hopefully, I can stall for time down here before house goons get surly."

Cole, Bill, and Ross walked over to the stair case at the opposite end of the bar, attempting to look unhurried. The revelers appeared to be largely ignoring the new men in the room. As they reached the bottom of the stairs two women, scantily clothed but well-covered with makeup, met them and followed alongside them as they climbed the stairs.

"You fellows looking for some fun upstairs," said the older of the two.

"We are after we link up with our friends in Baron Gerbold's party," replied Ross.

"Oh, the Baron left a few hours, ago. We hated to see him leave. He was interesting and quite generous," offered the younger woman.

"Did he leave with all his friends?" asked Cole.

"No, they are having a private party in one of the rooms. We were disappointed we were not invited."

"Maybe we can change their minds. We would want

you at our party," suggested Bill. "Take us to them and we will all have a roof-raising good time."

The older woman was fretful. "We really are not supposed to take you to their room ourselves and they said they were not to be disturbed. We don't want them mad at us. Here at The Haven people really mean it when they want privacy."

"Actually, our friends would be upset if we did not join them as soon as we arrived. I think you can understand that," said Cole and handed twenty dollars to the woman.

"Well, if you are sure, but if they are out of sorts, don't tell them we told you." She gestured at a door on the left near the top of the staircase. "We are two doors down. Come get us if you want us."

The last was said with a seductive purr that would have been more compelling if the woman had not leaned into Cole provocatively, overwhelming him with her ginny breath and a sweaty emanation masked by cheap perfume.

The three men stood by the indicated door and waited while the women entered their room farther down the hall. Cole waved and winked as they closed the door.

The men could hear voices inside. Cole cautiously tried the door, which was, as expected, locked. Ross pushed Cole aside and quickly picked the lock mechanism with some device he had in his coat pocket. Ross and Bill had pistols drawn as they rushed into the room.

Immediately before them an open window directed a desultory breeze about the edges of gaping heavy drapes.

At the edge of the windows two men in underwear sat at a card table with Chinese designs adorning the playing surface. An acrid odor filled the room.

Away from the window against an inside wall, a naked man vigorously swiveled his hips astride the pale body of a young woman, pinned beneath him on an incongruously expensive mahogany bed.

Cole growled gutturally and lunged at the bed. He grasped the man's neck with one hand and shoved his other hand and arm under the man's hips, lifting the surprised man, still copulating, off the woman and in one continuous motion swung him from the bed and pitched him head first out the open window.

The assault was so sudden that the victim reacted with a terrified shriek only as Cole plunged him through the open window. The young woman lay unmoved on the bed, eyes closed, making no attempt to cover herself. Cole stood looking at her silently for a moment with a mixture of relief and anxiety.

"That is Gladys Severn, Cole, a friend of Clover's. They appear to have her drugged or blind drunk," said Bill.

Ross turned from peering out the window and scowled at the men at the nearby table. "Where is Clover?" he asked menacingly.

A chubby, balding man stuttered, "I do not know. Honestly, I don't know. Please don't hurt me."

The second man exclaimed loudly, "Cole and Detective Ross. I was looking forward to your visit ,but I had no idea how stimulating your arrival would be. My companion was seated opposite the action and missed the full effect of Cole defenestrating the unfortunate Mr. Vicks. A technique often used in the middle ages, my dear Cole, but usually performed by a group of men.

"I will no doubt have to write about his singular display in one of my books. But really, old boy, tossing a man out like that, at full attention, we English might consider that a bit unsporting. I am not sure how my loyal readers will react. You Americans are so impulsive."

Cole and Ross stared at the effusive David Frame. "Oh, I might suggest, old man, basic hygiene, I really would wash my hands after that. It was a mite unsanitary. Merely a suggestion on my part of course."

Ross looked at Cole and snickered, "Don't let him draw you in with his clever ramblings, Ross," said Cole. "What ghastly thing are you smoking, Frame?"

"Hashish, old man, I do recommend it highly. I would invite you to share but my companion here appears to have wet himself at your spectacular entrance and besides we smoked it all." Frame laughed with an odd cackling that bordered on mania.

"Look, Frame, I detest you, but I won't hurt you if you cooperate. Where is Clover?" Cole asked with exasperation.

"She and the Baron left a few hours, ago. Came and went so to speak. All I know is that they were heading for the mountains. The Baron is punishing you for not giving him what he wants. He will amuse himself with your all too human emotions and confusion. He will teach you to rise above all that, to be the being you can become," taunted Frame.

"How are you to rejoin the Baron?" asked Cole.

"In Arkansas, in Hot Springs, but he will show when he is ready. Until he arrives, I will comport myself with my usual devotion to licentiousness. After all, I have an obligation to my followers." Frame cackled again until his face reddened and he began to cough and sputter.

"Look we better get out of here now or we will have to shoot our way out," broached Bill nervously.

"Bill's right, Cole, we are out of time, let's get Gladys and run for it," agreed Ross.

The poor girl had not moved an inch, lying thighs agape on the rumpled sheets.

"I looked around, her clothes are not in the room," said Bill.

Cole wrapped Gladys in the top sheet from the mattress and bundled her tightly in a thin blanket from the footboard of the bed. He tossed the roll over his shoulder and left the room without a look back at the still-laughing and coughing Frame.

At the top of the staircase, the three men saw an obviously heated altercation below at the bar between Alexander, a dour middle age man, and the young bartender.

As the group descended the stairs, the manager bellowed at them to stop while the bartender deftly pulled a shot gun from behind the bar. Before he could level it at the interlopers, Alexander had produced Colt 45s in each of his hands and snarled at the bartender and manager to put their hands on the bar and shut up.

The men positioned their hands as Alexander instructed, but the manager continued to curse Alexander and threaten him with vicious retribution from his many sources of protection, until Alexander cocked the Colts and thrust them closer to the men's chests.

"It is the here and now that counts, Mr. Brickley." Brickley looked back and forth several times at the Colts and Alexander's twisted smile and bulging eyes before gulping hard and looking as if he might faint.

By now the three men were down the stairs and Alexander began to follow as the group made their way outside. Alexander backed out of the room with his guns sweeping the perimeter as he walked. The partying horde, well besotted by now, and energized by the loud pulsating music, had been oblivious to the conflict until a woman screamed as Alexander edged out of the room with his gleaming pistols. The band stopped and the crowd noise reduced to a buzzing, murmuring cacophony.

As Alexander left the crowd's line of sight, he hollered, "Don't worry, Judge, these clowns will still vote for you."

Alexander ran sideways down the hall positioning himself so that a poorly aimed blast of the shotgun would not find him. Outside the house, the men bolted for the main, well-maintained path back to the beach. At the edge of the woods Cole foisted Gladys onto Bill's study shoulders.

"Head for the pier as fast as you can, signal the Captain for pick up, and don't wait for me. I will stay behind to prevent them from picking you off while you are exposed at the beach. I can swim out to you in the dark. I have exceptional night vision," ordered Cole.

"There are sharks," said Alexander.

"Unfortunately, life is full of human sharks as well. I am a tough chew for both kinds," Cole assured him.

Cole accepted one of Alexander's Colts and watched his friends trudge down the trail to the main pier. With the moon only occasionally breaking through the heavy clouds, Cole quickly adjusted to the near darkness and delighted, as usual, in the glowing vibrant night that came alive all around him with his enhanced sight.

He watched the house closely and, as expected, saw six men with weapons clump down the stairs from the porch. Cole fired a round above the lead man's head. Two of the group ran back inside the house. The other four spread out and began to shoot freely into the woods as they made for the overgrowth at both sides of the beach path.

Cole knew his pursuers had no idea how well he visualized them. He pinned them down with a series of well-placed shots that intimidated them from advancing from their poor sheltering positions.

Fortunately, Alexander had dropped a box of bullets in his pocket. Anytime one of the men shifted his position, Cole stopped him with several shots near his head and to his right and left. The men fired back at his position, homing on the flash from his weapon, but he moved enough to throw them off.

After a while, he scurried towards the beach along the edge of the path. At a twist in the path, he saw a clump of vegetation surrounded by a low metal fence with pike-like edging a few feet from the path. A powerful thrust to his left shoulder slammed him to the ground just short of the rectangular fenced mound. When Cole turned towards the sound of the blow, he found a grinning Frank Bowling staring down at him.

"Before you get up, Cole, you should know the Baron lets me drink of his blood, and I share many of your strengths. That's how I could sneak up on you. You were not looking for someone like yourself," elaborated Frank.

"The Baron has turned you?" asked Cole as he pulled himself to a seated position on the pine needle strewn ground.

Frank looked annoyed. "No, no transfusions. Just frequent draughts of his invigorating blood. The Baron promised he will complete my transformation, but he has failed to deliver up to now. Presently, I can do his bidding for daylight transactions, a useful subservient person for all his petty schemes."

"You do not sound happy with the present arrangement," commented Cole.

"I have seen the world through the eyes of your kind. I have to have the whole of it. I want to become one of the masters," replied Frank.

"There is more curse than blessing to this life. To walk in the day is a gift from God. Normal relationships with people are sacrificed and the lust for blood is a ghoulish torment," Cole sputtered angrily.

"You are a weakling, Cole, just as the Baron says. If you truly knew how to live, you would embrace your transformation, shrugging off frail human emotions and morality. You now are a creature framed to roam the world and take what you want. Unlike you, I am seizing what I need, creating my own transformation. I will take the blood you refused the Baron," Frank said.

Cole and Frank heard Cole's pursuers nearing their location. Frank stepped onto the path and fired four shots at the persistent cluster of approaching men. Painful wails erupted. Frank came back to the now standing Cole, saying laughingly, "They will leave us alone now, and best of all, they will blame you."

"What makes you think I will let you have some of my blood?" asked Cole.

Pointing his pistol at Cole's chest, Frank said, "I don't want some of it; I want it all. Drink some, drain the rest. Waste not, want not, you know." Frank laughingly waved a valise in his left hand.

"I will just slow you down a bit to make this easier on me." Before he could shoot Cole in the thigh to disable him, Cole and Frank heard a twig snap. One of the wounded pursuers was determined to have his vengeance and was raising a shotgun in preparation for a shot at Frank.

Frank speedily shot the man in the gut just as the shotgun let loose a ferocious blast at close range. Frank was propelled backwards and fell onto the low fence, impelled through the back by the pikes on the upper fence border.

The shotgun had macerated Frank's upper body and torn his throat so that he could only gurgle as he struggled against the pikes. Cole doubted Frank would survive more than a minute or two and wanted to continue on to the beach, but the smell of the blood overcame his revulsion. He opened the valise dropped by

Frank and, as expected, found bottles, large bore needles, and tubing.

With ironic justice, Cole slammed several hypodermic needles into Frank and watched the pulsating streams swish into the collection bottles. Within less than a minute, Frank's heart stopped.

Cole removed the needles, throwing them and the bottles into the valise, and strolled over to the man with the shotgun to confirm that he was dead.

When Cole returned for one last look at Frank, he noticed that the overgrown fenced enclosure was actually a small burial ground, probably no more than fourteen by six feet. Two worn tombstones told the story of two sailors from England who died of fever in the 1830s. No doubt the young men never expected to die so far from home and to be buried in such a lonely, forgotten manner.

Frank would not be buried here besides the ancient bodies, but there was a certain cosmic justice in his stained soul abandoning his material body in this isolated place.

Cole set out for the beach at a run, quickly finding the principle pier. Several row boats and a small motorized skiff were tied up on one section of the unguarded structure. Cole did not want to waste time trying to start the skiff and hopped into a row boat and briskly set out into what to normal eyes would be the impenetrable darkness of the open sea.

When the shore behind fell away, Cole signaled with his light in the general direction of the expected location of Captain Abraham. He got a return flash off to his right and made for his friends with powerful strokes of the oars.

Just short of his goal, he paused and opened Frank's valise. He drank the still-warm liquid ravenously and tossed the valise and all its contents into the sea. He had drunk the blood hastily and dribbled the liquid onto his shirt.

Wiping his mouth on his sleeve, he hastily brought the small boat alongside Captain Abraham's boat. Alexander and Bill had barely hoisted Cole aboard before Captain Abraham propelled his vessel at maximum speed out into open water.

"My God, Cole, you are covered in blood! Are you hurt? What happened back there?" asked Bill.

Cole had slumped to the deck and was nauseated both by the pitch of the vessel hustling through the water and the volume of blood he had just gulped down.

"I can't talk. Not my blood on clothes, Frank's blood. Let me lie here awhile," gasped Cole.

Cole lay as still as he could on the pitching deck, struggling to avoid regurgitating a stomach full of blood. Ross brought old work clothes from the Captain's locker, and the trio slowly stripped Cole of his ruined clothing and re-garbed him in the worn shirt and trousers of a hard-working fisherman.

They dumped his soiled clothing into the sea after covering Cole with a thick wool blanket, also courtesy of Captain Abraham's supplies.

After a while, Cole stopped pressing his face and fingernails into the deck and rolled onto his side. Ross placed another blanket under his head and squatted beside him. "What happened?" he asked.

"I had everything under control. Our pursuers were slowed down but unhurt. Then Frank surprised me. He had me down and was about to kill me. Frank had no problem killing our chasers. He shot several, but one got him with a shotgun. Knocked him into a piked fence. Blood was everywhere," answered Cole.

Cole could tell from Ross's face that he had additional questions about Frank's demise but had decided, for now, to allow Cole's simple explanation to suffice.

"I talked for a while with the Captain. We have a major problem. The girl will not manage a long automobile trip, and we will be a target as a group. The Captain says there is a seaplane at the other end of the harbor. A man out of Florida is trying to set up a regular flight service. He was in Cleveland and is heading back to Florida. We can try to make it worth his while to fly us back to Knoxville. Bill will take Alexander's car and follow backroads out of the state before heading back home," explained Ross.

"Nice plan but it hinges on the pilot's cooperation," said Cole.

"Alexander is very persuasive. If the plane is capable of flight, we will get home," emphasized Ross.

"We still do not have Clover," Cole stated wearily.

"There are no mountains here. They are where we are going; maybe Gladys can tell us something specific when she is better," Ross replied unconvincingly. He put his hand on Cole's shoulder. "We have to leave here right away and regroup our resources back in Knoxville. I am as frustrated as you are, but we are done here. It's time to go home."

"None of this would be happening if the Baron had not found me and wanted me under his thumb. Clover would not have been abducted and people would not be dead," Cole said with a quiver in his voice.

"Murderous scum are what they are. They cross the path of saints and sinners. You are not responsible for the Baron's deeds. Cole, you also have to accept the possibility that Clover is a willing participant in accompanying the Baron. She is a complicated, rebellious woman who likes to walk on the wild side. The Baron may not be forcing her to stay with him. He may have her mesmerized or even recruited her to his band of dark angels," cautioned Ross.

Cole's face was forlorn, but his voice was clear. "I do not have illusions about Clover's character or behavior, but I still have conviction that she possesses goodness and spirituality that she does not want presented to the rest of us. She wants so much to be an independent, emancipated woman that she has suppressed her natural womanly warmth."

Ross grasped Cole's shoulder for a few seconds but did not otherwise respond to Cole's declaration of faith.

"Just relax, we will be at the seaplane in a few minutes. No need to try to get up before then. The sun is about to rise. I will see if the Captain can provide me with some gloves, hat, and something to shield your face. Fortunately, I salvaged your sunglasses and that goo you put on your face from the clothing we jettisoned," Ross said.

Cole put the proffered glasses on his face and rolled back on his belly, praying that they would reach the harbor soon. In what seemed like near instantaneous response to Cole's pleading, the pitching vessel slowed and steadied. Cole crawled to the side and pulled himself up on the gunwale.

~

A faint light from the eastern horizon allowed Cole to see the distant dock where this miraculous flying boat was sheltered. He quickly forgot his nausea as the plane's shape sharpened within a light mist.

The peculiar machine had a form only a designing engineer with a strong motherly instinct could love. The little vessel appeared to be a high-wing strut braced monoplane, its engine mounted in a small enclosure atop the wing. What passed for a cabin attached directly in front of the wing, which Cole doubted spanned 40 feet. Twin tails adorned the fuselage which sat atop a large pontoon. Cole grew increasingly anxious as they docked near this odd device.

Ross examined Cole's face as he gave him gloves and a hat. "Don't worry. It's butt ugly and floats, perhaps it flies as well."

Alexander and Bill cautiously supported Gladys while they climbed unsteadily onto the dock. Gladys was now dressed in fisherman's gear with her wild hair shoved under a floppy wind-brimmed canvas hat. She was cooperative but gazed around with wild darting eyes.

Ross and Cole bade Captain Abraham goodbye and

thanked him for his kindness. The Captain stared at the girl and her escorts and gawked at the bizarrely garbed Cole.

"I will be happy to forget I crossed your path. I just regret that I did not drive a harder bargain for my services. There might be quite a few questions about your doings," the Captain said with a sly smile.

"The lack of an inquisitive mind and poor memory can get you out of a host of trouble in the world," suggested Ross.

The Captain laughed, clapped Ross and Cole on the back, and helped them off his vessel.

Alexander had already scurried into the tiny office on the small pier where the flying boat was secured, leaving Bill to support the weaving Gladys. The three men tacitly agreed that a beneficial outcome was best secured by not presenting themselves for review by their perspective pilot before he committed to the flight. In short order, Alexander joined them on the pier beaming with satisfaction.

"Our new friend is most pleased to have a lucrative diversion before jumping to his next stop. He will have you back in Knoxville in no time. We caught him eating his breakfast and ready to leave." Alexander had barely finished his sentence when a short man in a leather flying jacket strode out to meet them, his pilot's goggles swinging jauntily from straps around his neck.

"Gentlemen and Lady, may I present our illustrious pilot, former U. S. Army pilot, Lieutenant Brindle. He has graciously agreed to get you home in record time."

Brindle stopped short and could not prevent himself

from gaping at the odd assembly. Alexander must have given him some sort of rudimentary explanation for Cole's dress and Gladys's bewildered look and swaying posture. The good lieutenant quickly caught himself and addressed the business at hand after a perfunctory nod of his head in their collective direction.

"Alexander explained your need to secure medical assistance immediately back home in the bosom of your families. My only concern is that we should discuss a notable deficiency in my services. This is as you notice a flying boat. There are no wheels under that magnificent pontoon. I can only land on water. A lake or an accommodating river. Alexander wants me to land in Knoxville on the Tennessee River, but he also relates to me that the river is shallow and rough there and even small steamboats can only come up river after a nice rain.

"Fortunately, he says you have had good rains recently so I hope to find a stretch of water to permit a safe landing. If I cannot find a suitable puddle of water, then things become disagreeable for you, me, and my wonderful plane. With that said, I am ready to set out and I gather you are also."

Lieutenant Brindle directed them to a small plank bridging the pier and the plane, where a rope ladder dangled from the passenger cabin.

Two of the men positioned themselves at each end of the plank and held Gladys's hands as they guided her over the water onto the edge of the pontoon by the ladder. She was shaking badly, whether more from fright or withdrawal was arguable.

Bill lead the way to the passenger compartment with

one hand grasping Gladys's as she followed him upward. Climbing this way was tedious and Gladys was close to collapse as she was essentially pulled into the enclosure by Bill.

Cole quickly climbed up into the compartment where he found Bill and Gladys seated but gazing up at the sky. Gladys looked at each of them and said woefully, "It has no roof." And indeed, it did not. There were four seats and side panels with windows but a notable absence of a roof above their heads.

Lieutenant Brindle's ruddy face appeared at the top of the enclosure. Noticing their amazement, he laughed, "Don't worry, the sky's clear for now, and I have yet to have a bird poop on one of my passengers." He chortled hardily at his stock joke and handed them goggles after he instructed them on how to strap in. "Relax, we will be off in minutes. This is the only way to fly, with the wind romping through your hair. You will be begging me for another go before long."

True to his word, in short order, the engine spurted and Brindle's helpers had pushed his plane away from the pier to allow him to glide out into open water. With few boats in their vicinity, Brindle quickly lined up a stretch of water that appealed to him and opened the throttle.

The little plane bounced over the waves in an alarming fashion until, with a sudden swish, it launched into the air, climbing bumpily into the sky heading out to sea. When he had a comfortable altitude, Brindle banked his air boat and came around to a suitable course for their destination.

Alexander waved with great enthusiasm as they soared with an awesome roar over his head. Cross winds buffeting the little plane as they gained altitude. Soon, in spite of themselves, the passengers were gazing with awe at the green earth beneath them.

The weather was fine and the early morning light gave a special glow to the playhouse-sized farms, cattle, horses, and people they flew over. The few people out in their fields waved with abandon at the strange contraption soaring above them.

By the time a little of the novelty had subsided, they were into the clouds. Brindle skirted along the lower edges of the fluffy clouds, apparently not wanting to lose sight of earthly landmarks for too long.

Cole struggled with his clothing, self-consciously, constantly adjusting his covering to protect himself from marauder sunbeams. He was in constant fear that a gust of wind would dislodge his sun goggles or his scarves. In this enclosure, he could not protect himself if he lost any of his barriers to the sun. He feared his scorched skin would peel off and fly away into the trailing wind. Had he not fed several hours before this flight, he doubted that he could have controlled his panic. Eventually, he huddled down in his seat in a protective crouch, clutching his clothing tightly.

"Cole, Cole," Ross called and shook his arm. "Brindle's looking for a landing site."

Cole was startled that in his exhausted state he had slept through the majority of the flight, but even more frightened that he had not maintained total vigilance while they were in the air. He had the same sense of terror as if he awoke surrounded by dozing pit vipers who could have lurched and killed him at any time.

"Calm down, Cole, we are here," said Ross seeing Cole jerk and shiver in his seat. "Let's hope Alexander explained where we hope to alight from this flying bucket."

Brindle had come in near downtown and now followed the river at a low altitude assessing the depth and rockiness of the bottom as best as he could. He found some water that interested him and made several passes before he seemed satisfied.

Cole was mortified by this close up view of the rocks in the river's course. He did not doubt that Brindle's pontoon could float the river, but the initial powered plunge into the shallow river might ram them all into the bottom or into a malpositioned boulder.

Cole's fear of a solar roasting dissipated into a new panic as he imagined being crushed and drowned in this improbable flying boat. As Cole agonized, Brindle gained height and went past downtown and over Gay Street Bridge. Now, he turned back and made his angled approach to the narrow strip of water he had favored. Cole quickly realized that they were lined up to come in under the Gay Street Bridge.

"Ross, he's going in under the bridge," shouted Cole.

Cole's heart seemed to pause as he turned to Ross and observed his ashen face. Ross muttered, "And he is going under the elevated portion of the railroad bridge."

To the two men, the tips of the wings seemed too near the support beams and, if they cleared the Gay Street Bridge, the one section of the railroad bridge they must negotiate was so narrow that collision seemed inevitable.

Cole prayed and had little doubt that Ross was so engaged. A brief glance at Gladys found her with eyes closed, body trembling and rocking. Bill held her hand and spoke continuously to her in too low a voice for Cole to understand.

The little plane swooped under the street bridge, immediately tilted slightly left, and swept through the cut-out section of the trestle. The passage was so fast and smooth that Cole had no idea if they had feet or inches to spare.

Brindle had the plane down on the water in the time needed to level the plane. They lurched and bounced a couple of times before coasting smoothly along the river. Brindle stayed mid-stream and slowed to a leisurely pace. He craned his head over the fuselage trying to look for near surface obstacles. The glare from the sun made this examination suspect, and their slow progress was the only thing that might save them if they did strike a submersed obstruction.

Further along they came to several large houses on their right, some with docks and stairs leading up the hill to impressive structures. Bill shouted at Brindle to approach a particular dock of one of these homes. Brindle brought his plane to the dock dead slow and even brought it alongside the tiny pier.

A tall muscular black man tending the lower garden had watched the approaching vessel with awe and now walked over to assist. Brindle told Bill how to secure the flying boat with the vessel lines, which Bill and his new helper quickly secured to hooks on the pier posts.

The two men had pulled the flying boat to the edge of the pier and Brindle was able to get Cole, Gladys, and Ross off with no hesitancy on Gladys's part. Regardless of her nausea and trembling, the promise of being back on solid ground was such a powerful allure that she practically leaped from the flying boat onto the pier.

Bill addressed their good Samaritan, "We thank you for your help. I could not have pulled her in tight without your strong back. Isn't your name Jesse and isn't this Mr. and Mrs. Graywater's home?"

"Yes, Sir, and I mean no disrespect, but you are about the craziest folks I have ever seen. People won't believe me when I relate this to them," replied Jesse.

"I completely agree, Jesse, it would certainly be crazy to repeat that stunt. Are Mr. or Mrs. Graywater at home?"

"They were. It's a bit of a walk up the hill. The lady looks a little winded for that hike," said Jesse.

"Winded is a polite way to put it, but we do not have much choice do we," replied Bill.

"Guess not, sir," Jesse agreed.

Brindle spoke, "I thank you also, Jesse. Do you know where I can get aviation fuel?"

"Reckon not. Mr. Graywater might, though," replied Jesse.

"Well, we will just have to ask him then," said Bill and gestured for their little group to advance up the hill.

The twisting steep path was in good condition but

quickly left them loudly puffing with exertion. Ross and Bill stayed on each side of Gladys and gently pulled her upward by her arms. She was gasping and dry heaving by the time they reached the garden lining the patio overlooking the river. Both men felt like the worst sorts of gads but knew they had no choice but to get her up the hill immediately.

By now, Mrs. Graywater and her maid watched their approach.

"My servants informed me that some damn fools had landed an aeroplane on the river and come to visit me without an invitation, but I did not believe them. I thought they had found the key to the liquor cabinet again, but now I see that you are involved, Bill, so I should hardly be surprised. Who is that female with you she seems... Oh Lord, that is that sweet angel Gladys Fairfax. Don't just stare there, Delores, help them get her inside. What have you done to her, Bill? You are well-known as a rascal, but I never thought you would debauch a nice young girl like Gladys."

"I will try to explain inside your house, but we removed Gladys from the company of those who were despoiling her. We are rescuers, Mrs. Graywater," Bill countered.

Mrs. Graywater chortled, "Clearly an unfamiliar role for your Bill. I wager that Alexander is also involved in this misadventure."

"Indeed, Alexander was of great assistance in this delicate matter, Mrs. Graywater," said Bill.

"Well, you two rakes outwardly appear to be gallant gentlemen, as I often warn the mothers of our young ladies of society. For now, I will reserve judgment on whether you have actually turned over a new leaf."

Inside, Mrs. Graywater's ornate living room overlooked the winding river. Gladys sat on an overstuffed sofa trembling, face and neck mottled by the flush from her recent exertion. Mrs. Graywater's maid scampered back into the room with a glass of water.

"Careful with that, small sips only, she will certainly throw up more than a few mouthfuls," commanded Cole.

"And just who are you men?" demanded Mrs. Graywater, annoyed by someone giving orders in her house. Cole recognized that she had carefully avoided referring to them as gentlemen.

"I am Dr. Cole Sterling , this is Detective Ross and our pilot Lieutenant Brindle. I apologize for my appearance. I cannot tolerate any sunlight. I usually avoid venturing out in the day but we had no choice but to get Gladys back to Knoxville, to her family and for immediate medical care."

"Dr. Sterling, I have heard of you. I don't believe in all that mind mumbo jumbo, but I guess it is fine for those that do to partake of your services.

"You, Detective Ross, are always in the newspaper, not always glowingly, I might add," harrumphed Mrs. Graywater. She glowered at them, still unsettled by their unscheduled intrusion.

Cole ignored her snippy disapproval. "Please, Mrs. Graywater, do you know who acts as physician for Gladys and her family?"

"Well, I suppose I do since he is my physician also, Dr. Pride," Mrs. Graywater offered.

Cole thought to himself, *Thank God*.

"May I use your telephone to contact him about Gladys," asked Cole.

"Don't you think you should call her family first?" asked Mrs. Graywater.

"We can't afford to waste time to initiate treatment for Gladys, and Pride will do a better job of contacting her family than a stranger," explained Cole.

"Well, suit yourself. The device is in the vestibule," said Mrs. Graywater.

Cole pulled out his wallet, found Pride's number and gave it to the exchange. Pride's staff were efficient and had him on the telephone within no more than a minute.

"Ernest, this is Cole Sterling. I need your help. Can you come to the Graywater home right away and take charge of Gladys Fairfax. She has been raped, probably repeatedly, and is coming down from days of heroin or morphine administered along with I know not what else. She was abducted and I and friends of her family recently retrieved her. I do not have time to explain since I have to continue to look for another abducted young woman, but I would be most grateful if you could take over Gladys's care and notify her family of her whereabouts," Cole explained.

Cole was exultant that Pride was his usual taciturn, no nonsense self, and readily agreed to Cole's request after sputtering, "You damn well owe me a complete explanation along with a large whiskey at my club."

Cole was about to return to the others when he spun around and latched onto the telephone again, this time calling the Wainwright home. Cole once more felt favored by fortune. Catherine answered the telephone.

"Catherine, listen carefully, we did not find Clover, but did get Gladys Fairfax back. We have reason to believe that Clover may have been taken to the mountains. I think the Baron wants to continue to toy with me, so I am guessing that they are somewhere around here. Ross said I should ask you if your family has a getaway cabin."

"Yes, we have a cabin we own with another family in the mountains, a couple of hours drive from here," Catherine replied.

"It may be a wild goose chase, but I want to explore the possibility that the Baron took Clover there hoping for a repeat encounter with me. Can your father go with me right away?" asked Cole.

"No, he has been sick since Clover disappeared and now his gout has him bedridden. I will drive you up in my father's car. I will pick you up," said Catherine.

Cole explained where he was and hung up. He took Ross aside and elaborated his next move. Ross said, "I should go with you. If you are right, you are heading right into a trap."

"You need to stay here and use your contacts to look into other possibilities. We cannot afford to put all our resources on a long shot. Catherine and I can do this reasonably quickly. The Baron originally spoke of Hot Springs, Arkansas. See if there is any indication they have retreated there," said Cole.

"Cole, you are exhausted. We all are. You may not be able to defend yourself and Catherine. Wait until I can get someone to accompany you," Ross pleaded.

Cole rubbed his brow with one hand, his other hand on Ross's shoulder. "I appreciate your concern but this probably is a fool's errand and the quicker I close this door the quicker we can evaluate other possibilities."

Ross shrugged. "Suit yourself, but if you return without Clover, you have to start viewing this as a possibly lengthy war and stop rushing from skirmish to skirmish. Patience, judgment, and knowledge win wars," said Ross.

Cole laughed. "True, along with speed and brazenness."

Gladys was now in an upstairs bedroom and Mrs. Graywater and her maid were seeing to her needs as best as they could while awaiting Dr. Pride.

Catherine surprised Cole and rolled up in front of the Graywater home before Pride arrived. Ross said he would wait and give Pride what information they had about Gladys's circumstances.

Cole climbed in beside Catherine in her father's Cadillac sedan. He thought Catherine would let him drive while she directed, but she clearly had no intention of entrusting Cole with her father's beautiful, dark blue,mechanical wonder with its powerful V8 engine.

Cole had not had the privilege of riding in a Cadillac previously and was delighted by its smooth conquest of the road. He momentary forgot his concerns and enjoyed the swift progress of this sleek steel enclosure as they headed out of town.

Catherine drove with skill, and for a long time, she drove in silence.

After some time, Cole realized that he must have been sleeping. They were following a winding road far from any population centers. His fatigue and the hypnotic gentle bounce of the Cadillac had lulled him into a trance and then sleep.

Cole looked over at Catherine sheepishly. She smiled. "I could see you were all in. You drifted off right away, but now that you are with me again, you owe me the complete truth." She frowned at Cole. "I mean it, Cole, my sister is gone because of you. Why?"

Cole struggled inwardly before responding. "I have to start at the beginning for you to make any sense of it. What I will tell you will sound insane, but you must never share any of this with your family, not anyone. My career would be over whether people thought me mad, a liar, or a monster."

Catherine nodded her head in acceptance of Cole's terms. Cole continued, "During the war, my field hospital was overrun. I was taken to an aristocratic Frenchwoman's estate, where I was hours away from death, but the mistress of the house for reasons she could never well articulate decided to try to save me. She gave me a transfusion of her blood. Her blood had restorative and rejuvenative powers, and I recovered with startling speed, but my salvaged life was not the life I had before my injuries.

"I soon found that I could not tolerate the sun but that was counterbalanced by my heightened senses and by an increase in my overall strength. Regardless, my career as a surgeon was over. I could work only at night and operating lights would be too intense for me. My savior was a lay psychoanalyst taught by Professor Carl Jung. She trained me and secured his blessing for my career change," Cole looked at Catherine and could see she was puzzled.

"So, you wonder how is this narrative going to lead to the Baron's obsession with me?" Cole asked. "The missing link is the fact that Aurora, my savior, teacher, and eventually my lover could not survive without drinking blood. When she figuratively resurrected me, I became similarly cursed. My food needs are minimal, but I absolutely cannot survive without blood to drink. Like Aurora, I prefer human blood.

"In France, we could purchase a small supply. The remainder of the time we made do with animal blood, which is my sustenance now. Aurora had saved one other person, her ex-husband, Marie-Henri Cartan, who after his transformation became a sick, sadistic degenerate who satiated himself with sex, drugs, and human blood.

"The Baron who revels in human degradation, took Cartan under his wing and first introduced him to the world of depravity he came to occupy. The Baron had Cartan transform him so that he could dominate his innocent victims far beyond his previous manipulations. As much as he enjoyed his new power, he soon realized that being unable to walk openly in the day was far more limiting than he imagined.

"Cartan had told him that Aurora's grandfather could walk in the sun when he wished and the Baron believed that if he could have some of Aurora's blood, that somehow he might acquire her grandfather's abilities.

"In his mind, Aurora's blood in combination with the strength of his formidable will would recreate the potency of her grandfather. Cartan probably was to get Aurora's blood for the Baron, but instead he killed her and vanished.

"Now, the Baron apparently believes that because I am not deranged like Cartan, that my blood may have the potency that combined with his, will give him the gift of day walking or, at least, enhanced powers."

Cole stopped and waited for Catherine to respond to his monologue. During his speech, Catherine's face fleetingly flickered from amazement to horror to disbelief, and now a struggle to avoid crying.

Cole turned toward Catherine, his eyes downcast, seemingly staring at his gloved hands. "I am clad so that no part of my body is touched by the sun. A hat, a balaclava over my face, sunglasses, all part of an alien appearance, a subhuman telling you a story that is unbelievable and, if believed, make me an unnatural monster. You cannot look over at my facial expressions or into my eyes as I tell you how I came to be here today with you."

Cole slumped against the car door and listened to Catherine crying. After a while, Catherine reached for his hand and held to it tightly until she needed to return it to the steering wheel.

"I have never heard of anything like your condition, Cole. I will not say that I believe all you have said, but I trust you, and know there must be something of the truth in what you are telling me. Are you saying that the Baron is using Clover to blackmail you into giving him what he wants?" asked Catherine.

"Yes, but he also wants to break my spirit. He wants to dominate me as he does his followers and have me with him as he continues his dark passage through the world," Cole responded.

"He sounds pure evil," said Catherine.

"His actions and intentions are evil. I do not know enough about the man to know if he was always so or if some spark of humanity still resides in his being. Regardless, he is very dangerous and I believe that he will kill to get whatever he wants." Cole paused. "He may also kill just for the thrill of it."

Their trip into the hills had been slowed by the twisting rough roads and the Cadillac's engine at times struggled with the incline. Catherine seemed relieved to point at a country store at an approaching intersection. "We will turn here. My family's cabin is not too far." Catherine pointed at the nearby stream. "The road follows the creek. There is a cluster of cabins near the water."

Soon Catherine slowed the Cadillac to a crawl as she crossed a disreputable, creaky wooden bridge over the creek. The Cadillac was a tight fit and the plank bridge groaned with its weight.

"I am glad you are petite, otherwise, we might be in the water right now," said Cole.

Catherine laughed, "Well, it is true that we never cross with more than two in the car."

The sun was dropping fast behind the hills and the woods seemed ominously dark. Catherine drove very slowly along the pitted dirt road toward a cluster of cabins. She did not use her headlights and she stopped the vehicle about a hundred yards short of the nearest cabin.

"Look, there are lights in our cabin." Catherine edged the car a little closer and turned into a small open space between tall trees. "I will park here. I do not think you want to drive up to the door."

"No, an element of surprise might be nice," said Cole.

"Sarcasm is merely rudeness in disguise, Dr. Sterling,"

"I apologize profusely, Miss Wainwright," Cole replied.

"More sarcasm belies your apology, Doctor. I could take my motorcar back to Knoxville," Catherine teased.

"Joking aside, since they do appear to be holed up in your cabin, I realize that means I have now put you in danger along with Clover. Please let me go in while you go for a constable," said Cole seriously.

Cole had his hand on Catherine's during his exhortation. She grasped his hand and stated emphatically, "Cole, I am going in with you now. Clover is my sister. In spite of your guilt, this is not your fault. Somehow you may need me to make this right."

Cole began to protest. Catherine put her finger on his lips and shook her head no. She opened her door and got out quickly.

The moon was now behind the clouds. The cabin light was a beacon in the darkness but did not illuminate the obstacles between the car and the cabin. Cole took Catherine's hand and said, "I will guide you through the woods. Step high and carefully."

The two advanced slowly through the brush. They traced a jagged path as they avoided the larger bushes, brambles, and depressions in the forest floor. Catherine had dressed in her best tomboy fashion, but was still not well protected from scratches and sticks from innumerable small obstacles.

Cole saw clearly in the darkness, but their progress was slowed by the need to guide Catherine around larger obstructions. As they drew near the cabin, Cole could see an automobile up against one end of the elevated front porch.

A large man leaned on the hood of the vehicle, a cigarette clinched between his lips, the glowing tip illuminating his face with every lingering draw of the smoke into his lungs.

Cole whispered to Catherine of the man's presence. She pointed to steep, narrow stairs on the side of the cabin, which was the only other access into the structure. They went up the steps and slowly opened the door a few inches.

The guard was looking away from the back of the house and, fortunately, did not see the dim light that tumbled from the crack in the door as they squeezed into the cabin.

Once inside they stood, still holding hands, as they took in the interior. Cole sucked in his breath at the sight of a young woman in a sheer peignoir near the center of the cabin. She stood one hand resting on a table next to the wall. A single oil lamp on the table lit the one-room cabin, trans-illuminating the thin women's peignoir evoking the image of a fragile waif.

Catherine uttered a barely audible cry and ran to the woman, spinning her around, throwing her arms around her neck. Cole had not moved, smiling as he recognized Clover. He started as a familiar voice came from a dark corner of the cabin.

"I told Clover you would be here soon." The Baron strolled from the shadows, a pistol in his right hand, a short sword in his left.

"Were you expecting a mob, Baron, you seem well prepared?" observed Cole.

"I heard of your escapades with your friends and prepared accordingly. Now here you are with a slip of a girl as a companion. Move aside, please." The Baron waved Cole and Catherine away from the table.

There were two chairs a few steps from the table. The Baron ordered the two to sit. Clover had not really moved. She looked at all of them impassively, the pupils of her eyes tiny black specks. The Baron placed the short sword on the table, maintaining the pistol pointed at Cole's chest.

"I never travel without my short sword. I survived the war because of it. My father had it made for me by a firm that had made swords for our soldiering family for hundreds of years," said the Baron.

"Right now, the sword is not impressing me, but the pistol aimed at my chest is," said Cole.

"Merely to prevent any vituperative disagreement. I

hope to quietly convince you of the acceptability of my position."

"After you abducted and debased two young women merely to spite me and perhaps compel me to give you what you want,"

"It is a modern world, Doctor. Sensuality and broadened perspectives are here to stay. The women were not entirely innocent. They just received a more explosive, comprehensive experience than they bargained for. I must also correct you in another detail. I do not want to have your blood. I need your blood. There are profound changes at work in my homeland. The humiliation leaped upon Germany is over-whelming my hard-working compatriots. Without the ability to once again be a day-walker, I cannot take my place as a leader in my country to right this historical outrage and restore it to its rightful place at the head of nations."

"You must know there is little chance my blood will have the effect you want. Aurora could not tolerate the sun, only her grandfather could. We have no knowledge of how he came to be the way he was. Assuming that Aurora's converts could somehow mingle their blood and recreate the prototype is fanciful," stated Cole.

"There is powerful scientific work in progress in Germany with genetics and immunology. I believe it is possible to find the right combination that will work," argued the Baron.

"Even if your premise is valid, there is a remote chance that I just happen to be the right match to achieve your goal, Baron. It seems merely obsessive of you to go to such lengths for such a tenuous possibility," said Cole.

"Remote or not, you will comply," the Baron said as he swept the pistol barrel back and forth between Cole and the women. "To illustrate my magnanimity and my confidence in your arrival today, I drew some of my blood and kept it iced in anticipation of your imminent visitation."

The Baron bent over and removed an ice bucket from under the table while ostentatiously continuing to cover Cole with the pistol. Several water glasses were inverted on a cloth on the table. The Baron removed the lid on the bucket and withdrew a crimson flask from which he poured a generous aliquot of blood into one of the glasses.

"I insist, my friend. You must be quite thirsty after your trials and tribulations. Here, I do insist," the Baron emphasized as he extended the glass to Cole. "I apologize ladies that I do not have a suitable beverage for you. There is a bit of wine here somewhere. After Cole and I conclude our business, I will attempt to rectify my omissions as your host."

Cole took the glass and sniffed its contents. "Oh, don't be so suspicious, Doctor. The glass has only fine German aristocratic blood and an excellent vintage, if I do say so myself. Please enjoy it. Savor it. Sadly, it won't keep," the Baron explained.

As tempting as it was to throw the glass in the Baron's face, Cole decided that prudence required capitulation for now. He sipped the liquid. "I could claim your bodily fluid was as disgusting as you and your obsession, but I am too tired to want to banter with you. The blood is excellent. I will happily drink it to revive myself, but I still do not want to reciprocate with my blood."

"Oh, but you will, my dear fellow. You will not want me to shoot you or one or both of these fine ladies," warned the Baron.

Cole finished drinking and sat the glass on the table.

"Why is Clover still standing? What have you done to her?" Catherine asked tearfully.

The Baron reached again under the table, lifted a flat metal box, and removed the contents, which were positioned on a hand towel on the table's surface. Two large syringes, several needles, an elastic band, and adhesive plasters were fastidiously oriented by the Baron as he answered Catherine.

"She is merely in a special place in her mind. I have an interesting concoction I have developed after much experimentation. Clover is enjoying its effects; standing is of no concern to her. In fact, most everything is of no concern to her. Now, Cole, move your chair adjacent to the table and we will begin. Alas, because I must obtain your continued cooperation with this weapon, I cannot assist you. Fortunately, as a physician, you can manage on your own."

Catherine said in a clear but low voice, "If you are low enough to do this to my sister, why should we believe that you will not kill us all after you get the blood?"

"Think, my dear. If I intended murder, I would have shot the three of you and ,without the current drama from you, drained Cole of every tasty drop. I intend to keep Cole for a while. If drinking the blood does not work, I will try injecting it perhaps in different ways. I was trained as a soldier and a scientist in the service of my Kaiser. Training that has served me well."

"Come, come, come, Cole, move. My patience is flagging," ordered the Baron.

Cole rose and moved his chair close to the edge of the table. He sat and stared at the Baron.

"You are trying my patience. Put your arm on the table and use the compression band. I know you can insert the needle and draw a syringe of blood with one hand," said the Baron.

Cole positioned his arm and applied the band, but then stared at the Baron, who was visibly agitated by Cole's delays. He leaned across the table thrusting his pistol against Cole forehead. The Baron's intense focus on the recalcitrant Cole, blinded him to Clover's sudden movement, snatching the Baron's sword from the table, and in a smooth arc, severing his extended pistol hand.

Catherine screamed along with the Baron, who followed with a screech and howl as his arm delivered a pulsing gush of blood into Cole's face.

The Baron wobbled on his feet momentarily then rushed to the front door of the cabin, howling as he ran with his right arm clutched tightly against his chest.

Cole wiped blood from his eyes, as he rose from the chair and located the Baron's pistol on the floor before running to the door. He heard the car's engine crank. He turned back inside and saw Catherine clutching Clover and crying while Clover stood impassively.

"See if she will lie down with you on the cot," Cole said.

"You do not think they will come back?" asked Catherine.

"Not right away, but I also do not think we should try to drive out right now. We will leave at first light. I will sit on the porch in the dark with the pistol while you rest with her."

Cole turned the oil lamp down to minimize the light from the cabin and wiped his face with a cloth from the Baron's box before returning to the porch. He pulled a capacious wooden rocking chair into the ideal position to view the major approaches to the cabin. He sat near the edge of the porch and watched the clouds float across the face of the moon with a sprinkling of stars obstinately twinkling in spite of the best efforts of the shifting bundles of clouds.

He watched an owl swoop down on a little mouse scurrying through the brush and thought how close he had come to being in the clutches of a predator. The association of the presence of evil with the reencounter with the Baron, and the feeling of powerlessness to protect Clover and Catherine merged into intense melancholy as he was overwhelmed by images from Aurora's death.

He grieved again for the loss of her loving presence and relived his shame and humiliation at being unable to save her. Cole sobbed in shaking surges until finally exhausted with his head cradled in his hands. He eventually leaned back in a corner of the rocker with his arms wrapped around him and his eyes closed with the moonlight painting his drawn features.

"Cole, Cole, wake up. It is near full light. You are sitting in the sun. You are not burning," said Catherine with the last words nearly a whisper.

Cole opened his eyes and gasped at the trees dazzling him with their green leaves and the gurgling stream flooding his vision with silvery flashes. He stood a gruesome, severe figure, and took in everything around him with Catherine holding tight to his arm.

They both heard the lumbering truck approaching the cabin followed by a shiny black Ford. "That looks like Constable Bill's truck," said Catherine.

As the vehicle drew closer Catherine recognized her father in the Ford and waved with delight. The constable climbed out of his truck first and approached them cautiously. Cole noticed his hand stayed near his holstered weapon, the strap unsnapped and dangling.

"If I had not been told who you are, I would put you down as an axe murderer," said Constable Bill with a pronounced Southern drawl as he took in the coating of dried blood on Cole's shirt and similar smudges in his hair, face, and ears.

Catherine ran down the stairs to her father. "Daddy, we have Clover. We are all safe. Come see," she said excitedly.

Catherine bubbled her narrative as she led her father, the constable, and the apparent owner of the Ford into the cabin. Cole could not bear to go back inside and continued to appraise his new condition.

He left the porch to get the full sun on his face and

hands, even pulling his pant legs up to expose his pale lower legs. No part of his skin reddened, blistered, or pained him. The Baron's ridiculous hypothesis was working, at least for him, for now. Cole realized that even if the Baron had obtained his blood, whatever effect was at work might not have cured the Baron. None of the Baron's other attempts had helped him.

The sad final conclusion of his ruminating was that this experience might not last. Without regular exposure to the Baron's blood, Cole might revert to his past state, forced to live in the darkness.

Cole tried to be philosophical and accept that he would enjoy this reprise while it lasted and take solace in the knowledge that a treatment even if poorly understood, did exist.

The men came out of the cabin, Jake Wainwright supporting his recovered daughter on one side and the driver of the Ford clutched her on the other. The constable carried the Baron's box along with the blood-tinged short sword.

Jake paused when even with Cole. "I suppose I should thank you, Doctor, but since I surmise this business was instigated by your presence, I am a little short of gratitude right now."

Cole did not respond to the reproach but said, "Please, do not take Clover home. Take her to Doctor Ernest Pride. He will get her safely through withdrawal."

Clover looked at Cole tearfully and sadly before getting into the back of the Ford with her father.

"Aren't you going with your sister? I can drive your father's car back alone," Cole said to Catherine.

"No, I told them you were ill and needed me to get us home."

The constable came alongside them. "I need that bulge in your coat pocket, Cole. Evidence, you know. Fortunately for you, Catherine is a good witness and I hear you are a good friend of Detective Ross. All that carries a lot of weight with me. By the way, if you see that Baron tell him I have his hand in his box, fits right nicely."

As the constable climbed into his truck, Cole hollered out, "I want that sword back when you are done with it. I intend to return it to the Baron at some point." Constable Bill smiled and waved as he pulled away from the cabin.

Cole looked at Catherine. "Kind of a laconic fellow."

"Not if you make the mistake of getting him started on catching crappie or trout," replied Catherine,

"How did the constable and your father come to be here this morning?" Cole asked.

"Apparently, there are some people in some of these other cabins. They were puzzled by the strange car and the scary driver. The commotion last night got them to call the constable at dawn and my father rolled up at his house just before he left to come up here," said Catherine

"I thought your father was sick."

"He is recovering well from his gout. He is a little perturbed at me. Another reason I did not want to ride back with him. I did not get permission to take his car. He had to get his friend Gary to bring him when Mother confessed we had come up here," said Catherine.

"You are a depraved woman, Miss Catherine," said Cole.

"Maybe we can discuss my wicked ways someday over a nice picnic up here," suggested Catherine.

"I assure you I never want to see this cabin again, but I will be happy to picnic with you somewhere closer to home, Chilhowee Park, perhaps," replied Cole.

Catherine kissed a non-blood smeared patch of Cole's cheek.

"That may work out just right, Doctor, on some nice sunny day."

PART THREE

Washington D.C. 1934

Cole walked slowly out of the hotel lobby into the shadow of the porte-cochere . He stopped a few feet from the revolving lobby door and dabbed a small amount of zinc oxide on his nose before positioning sunglasses on the bridge of his nose. He peered around, seemingly evaluating the weather, while locating the two men who had made a brief appearance at his presentation. They sat inside a Ford parked halfway around the curved driveway. Cole strolled toward them. As he expected, the men glanced at each other as they realized that he was purposefully engaging them.

"Good afternoon, gentlemen. I had the honor of your presence at my talk, but you left too quickly to have garnered any of my great body of wisdom. I was either more tedious than usual or you only entered the room to be able to identify me afterwards. Since I am sure that the latter was your mission, I am making it easy for you to meet me for whatever purpose you have in mind."

"You are Dr. Cole Sterling, formerly Captain Cole Sterling of the American Expeditionary Force in France, are you not?" asked the Ford's driver, a young man in a poorly pressed suit.

"I am indeed, but I doubt you really questioned that," replied Cole.

The man in the car's passenger seat said, "We would like to meet with you Captain Sterling. We are with the U.S. Army's Military Intelligence Division. We need your assistance. If you will join us, we will talk as we go for a short drive."

"Sorry, my mother was quite clear about the perils of riding with strangers. I tell you what I will do. Lafayette Square is right over there. I am going for a nice walk around the White House. We can tarry on a bench in the park while you explain to me why you believe you need my assistance."

The younger man began to protest but stopped abruptly when his passenger placed his hand on his arm. He shrugged and eased his lanky frame out of the vehicle while his partner waved over a bellhop, who scowled at the proffered identification as he realized there would be no tip for watching over the Ford. The two men followed Cole as he worked his way over to the square, where he selected a park bench shaded by a large tree. Cole made a point of sitting at one end of the bench so the men could not bracket him between them.

" Do you mind if I have a look at the identification you flashed at the bellhop?" asked Cole. Both men handed over leather badge covers for Cole's examination.

"Well, Captain Bell and Lieutenant Scott you have whetted my interest in what you require of me. I did not even know there was an active Military Intelligence Division in the peacetime Army."

"The Division had various titles and responsibilities immediately prior to and during the war. Today we provide many services, one of which is to act as a repository of intelligence information from around the world. The primary reports are provided by military attaches assigned to foreign embassies. The attaches were originally in Paris, London, Berlin and Moscow. They are now located around the globe. Unfortunately, the attaches' reports are often ignored both by their own ambassadors and by the War Department General Staff here in Washington. However, some attaches know how to elicit some urgency about specific subjects. This has recently occurred with a report from our attache in Berlin. He reports that a German SS officer wants us to assist his and his family's escape from Germany along with a scientist who also wishes to escape the Nazis," explained Captain Bell.

"Why do they need your help? I did not think the Nazis have the country locked down that tightly," asked Cole.

"An SS officer working in a sensitive area is always

under suspicion. He would find it impossible to take his wife and child out of the country without an ironclad justification. The scientist is closely watched and would never get across the border under any circumstances," responded Lieutenant Scott.

"The diplomatic melee that would erupt if the American embassy was implicated in this would be career ending for everyone involved. Why would you even consider this? We are not at war with Germany, Thank God" said Cole.

" That is where the rest of the story comes in. This SS officer oversees a research facility that evaluates deadly diseases for potential as weapons. This effort is not new. The Germans had a clandestine facility at the start of the last war where they worked on Anthrax to use against the transport horses and livestock of their enemies. Currently they have active research with bacterial and viral specimens. Some of their agents travel to South America, Africa, and the Soviet Union to collect samples that may be useful for germ warfare."

"The scientist who wants to escape has been working on a deadly virus that causes blistering, bleeding and death in nearly all who are exposed to it. He also claims to have nearly perfected a vaccine to protect anyone exposed to the virus. He wants help in retrieving samples of the organism and the vaccine. Then he will continue his work here in the United States under military direction. "

Captain Bell paused in his narration as an attractive young woman walked by the park bench with a staccato clatter of high heels. She appraised the three men, passing them with poorly suppressed disdain.

Bell said sotto voce "Do not dismay, gentlemen. She was not evaluating our masculine good looks. This is Washington D. C. She was assessing our probable power quotient. We apparently failed in that regard, presumed by her to be mere cogs in the machine. Oh well, where was I? Ah, yes, our scientist, SS officer and family and samples need to be extracted from an increasingly locked down and hostile Germany," continued Captain Bell.

"I hope I look perplexed, As entertaining as this wild story is, I cannot even remotely see how any of this involves me. I have never been to Germany and know nothing about rare infectious diseases. What do you believe I can do that is critical your mission?" interjected Cole.

Bell and Scott exchanged glances nervously. " The SS Officer in this case wants you to come to Germany to help him remove the samples from the research facility. To get the samples out of this high security laboratory requires unusual abilities, which he claims you possess," replied Bell. Cole sat up abruptly.

"Who is this SS Officer?" asked Cole.

" Baron Werner Gerbold"

Cole bolted from the park bench, startling a passing older man causing him to stumble. Cole gesticulated wildly as the two men tried to maintain impassive expressions.

"Are you insane? The man is a threat to civilized people. He has abducted young women. If he is not a murderer, he has certainly abetted murder. I suspect his involvement in my fiancee's death. He kidnapped and debauched young women in my new home town and blackmailed and threatened me as I tried to save one of these women. I am sure he blames me for the loss of his hand at our last encounter. If this man wants me in Germany, it is to torture, humiliate and kill me, not to escape his homeland. How telling that he is now an SS officer in charge of germ warfare for a dangerous regime that is persecuting many of its own loyal citizens. I do not see how you can believe anything that he is reporting."

Cole had been shouting, stopping abruptly as he recovered his sense of his surroundings.

He stood completely still as he said quietly, "You cannot believe this man. I will not participate in an enterprise this dangerous based on Gerbold's assurances."

Cole sat down. He was nauseated, emotionally drained and covered in perspiration.

Bell remained silent while Cole slowed his breathing. "We do not know the full extent of your encounters with Gerbold. Those who might know will not talk to us, but we have seen the Interpol reports about Gerbold, as well as the Belgian police reports related to the death of your fiancee. We do understand Gerbold has a history as a devious, wicked degenerate who has been clever enough to stay out of the hands of the police. He claims to have joined the Nazi party to insulate himself from repercussions from his past misdeeds. He also claims to have reformed in recent years, regret his past behavior and now only wishes to protect his wife and child."

Cole's face was distorted with rage, but before he could unleash another tirade, Bell continued, " We have independent confirmation of his assertions about the existence of the virus. As you probably know, once Hitler took control, he began to persecute the Jews. Even many Jews thought his policy was limited and for show, finding it difficult to believe that productive loyal citizens, many who fought in the war for Germany would be earnestly persecuted by the new regime."

"As time has passed, the seriousness of their situation has been accepted by most Jews. Some of the Jewish scientists who were employed at the Baron's facility were dismissed within the last few months. A few cautiously reached out to interlocutors who provided our Berlin attache with information that validates Gerbold's claims. These scientists had become very nervous within the last year about what the Nazis would do with the dangerous organisms that the military had stockpiled."

Lieutenant Scott spoke for the first time since they entered Lafayette Square. "What makes Gerbold believe that you have unique abilities to help him remove materials from a high security instillation run by the military? "

Cole stared at both men for a while before he decided to answer Scott.

"You have seen my file. You know I was mortally wounded in France and survived due to receiving a blood transfusion from the woman who became my fiancee. I healed quickly from wounds that should have killed me, but I paid a high price. I could no longer tolerate sunlight, ending my career as a surgeon. The transformative blood gave me unusual physical strength, speed and heightened senses. Gerbold undoubtedly believes, or wants you to believe, that I can utilize those advantages to succeed in removing the laboratory samples without detection."

"Yet, here you are, sitting in the sun without difficulty," objected Lieutenant Scott.

"At my last encounter with Gerbold, he forced me to drink his blood in the bizarre belief that it might cure the toxic response to sunlight that I had endured for four years. He intended to force me to give him some of my blood to cure him of the same malady . He ended up having his hand severed before he could force me to part with my blood, Oddly, his crazy hypothesis worked, at least for me. I am still sensitive to sun exposure , but I am not prevented from having limited exposure in the day ," replied Cole.

"That answer left me with at least a hundred questions, but we are not here to fully understand your condition. "said Bell.

"We know that you were examined in France by multiple doctors and by a very suspicious Colonel, who ultimately facilitated your discharge from service in 1919 while you were still in France, a very unusual decision. There is no record of your new abilities, but the record is clear about your wounds, incredible recovery and the severity of your response to direct sunlight, On behalf of the War Department General Staff, I am formally asking you, Captain Sterling, to undertake this mission."

"Before you respond, I have a specific message to you from Gerbold. He understands that you do not trust him, but if you agree to help him, he will tell you where to find a man by the name of Marie-Henri Cartan. He will give you this information once you are in Germany. If you decide the mission is too dangerous after you have all the details, you are free to leave to pursue this Cartan without any interference from him."

The forlorn Cole seemed to Bell to be struggling for a response. He stared at Bell angrily as if to say how could you do this to me.

" Regardless of how I feel about this enterprise, there are practical considerations. I am going home tomorrow. There are patients who depend on me. I cannot abruptly take off for Germany," Cole declared.

"We have anticipated your concerns. We intend for you to leave tonight. An experienced Army psychiatrist is prepared to leave tomorrow for Tennessee to attend your patients in your absence for as long as required," responded Bell.

"Does that include taking over for me after Gerbold kills me slowly? " asked Cole caustically.

"You will return, Captain Sterling. Gerbold needs you alive."

" Well then, the Nazis may enjoy dispatching me," growled Cole.

"Lieutenant Scott will drive you to New York tonight. You will leave tomorrow on the fastest ship running the Atlantic crossing. You will disembark in France and then fly from Paris to Berlin where Gerbold will meet you. There is a psychiatry conference, fortuitously, which will be in session by the time you reach Berlin. The cover story is that you will attend this meeting and will be hosted in Germany by your old friend Baron Gerbold."

Cole lifted his eyes to the sky. " Heaven help me, you intend for Gorbold and me to pretend to be old friends!"

"Do you really work for the General Staff or for Lucifer? I would be hard pressed to concoct a more diabolic predicament for a soul who has been previously tormented by the likes of Gerbold."

Cole stood." I have had more sun than I can tolerate. Lieutenant ,when do you intend to pick me up at my hotel?"

"Actually, Sir, I will accompany you to the hotel. We will leave as soon as you collect your things,"answered Scott.

Cole gaped at the young Lieutenant before shrugging resignedly and setting out for the hotel. He turned abruptly, planting himself face to face with Captain Bell. "Just what would you have done if I had flatly refused this trip?"

"Army Officers are subject to recall when needed, Captain," Bell replied with a frosty smile.

Berlin 1934

The airplane arced over the center of Berlin, giving Cole an impressive view of the city center as the sun disappeared over the horizon while the pilot lined up for his final approach to Templehoff before landing smoothly on a grass runway. Inside the terminal, Cole stood in line with his suitcase at customs when he was surprised by a young SS officer in an immaculate uniform, who politely said,

" Please, Herr Doctor Sterling, allow me to carry your bag and take you around these lines."

Cole surrendered his luggage and followed the young man to a desk at the side of the custom's area. An official there gave a cursory glance at Cole's passport while he recorded the passport number, then waved Cole and his escort through into the main terminal, where a beaming Baron Gerbold embraced Cole while whispering into his ear.

" We are watched, smile. It is not safe to talk seriously here."

Cole made an effort at a smile while Gerbold walked at his side with his arm on Cole's shoulder.

"How was your trip? You had the pleasure of seeing our entrancing metropolis from the air. Quite impressive, don't you think? The city is much brighter now. More light, festive banners, shabby buildings painted. Even in a brief time, the new regime has begun the transformation of our beautiful city. There are great plans at work." said Gerbold as they walked.

Cole assumed that much of this effusive monologue was for the benefit of the young SS man at their side. A new Mercedes sedan waited at the curb outside the terminal. After placing Cole's bag in the trunk, the Baron's aide sat up front next to the driver, who was also attired in an SS uniform. The Baron kept up a monologue about the airport and what sights they would pass on the way to their destination.

"Have you arranged a hotel room for me near the conference?" asked Cole.

"I would not dream of having you stay in a hotel. You are a guest in my home. My wife is eagerly looking forward to your visit. She has heard so much about you. A handsome American psychiatrist as a house guest. Her friends are jealous, "Gerbold replied.

Cole restrained himself in front of their fellow passengers.

"I really hate to put you and your wife out on my behalf. I assumed that I would stay in a hotel near the meeting."

"Oh, this is much better. I cannot disappoint my wife, and we can talk about old times much better in the comfort of my home," Gerbold insisted.

Cole detected a slight emphasis on the word talk.

"In that case, I look forward to meeting your family. Certainly, we have a lot to discuss and no doubt you are correct that the comfort of your home is ideal for us to catch up with each other lives," Cole responded, continuing the pretense of congeniality in front of their minders.

The Baron visibly relaxed with Cole's active participation in the charade. He returned to the role of genial tour guide as their driver cruised by a number of notable sights in central Berlin before he delivered them to the Baron's villa in Wilmersdorf. The Baron dismissed his driver and aide after giving instructions for their morning duties.

" You certainly live well, Baron. This is a very grand home on impressive grounds," said Cole.

"In my wife's presence, you need to call me Werner, Cole. After all ,we are claiming that we are old friends," cautioned Gerbold.

The front door opened with a delighted squeal as the Gerbolds' daughter ran to her father, who scooped her up into his arms.

The Baron's wife, blond, beautiful, wearing a well tailored white silk blouse and black skirt, followed her daughter. Gerbold introduced his dear friend Cole.

"I am pleased to meet you Baroness,"said Cole.

"Call me Anneleise, please Cole. I cannot have my husband's old friend call me Baroness."

"Your English is excellent, Anneleise,"said Cole.

"Thank you, I know I have a strong accent, but I believe you will understand me well enough. Please come inside. The wild child in my husband's embrace is Ilse.

As they entered the atrium, Cole said, "You are a very beautiful girl, Ilse . You are the image of your mother, but I am sure you have been told that many times."

Ilse's mother translated Cole's statement. Ilse blushed and hid her face on her father's chest.

"Thank you," Ilse replied in English.

"Her tutor is teaching her English. Your visit will, no doubt, motivate her to take her studies more seriously."

"Anneleise, I need some time alone with Cole in my study before dinner. Could we join you for dinner in half an hour?" asked Gerbold.

"Of course, I will see that everything is ready." The

Baron placed Ilse on the floor, kissed her and her mother on the cheek and directed Cole into an adjacent room.

"Please sit there near the fireplace. I will join you as soon as I put Mozart on the phonograph. I think you will enjoy the fidelity of my speakers. Would you care for a brandy? I certainly need one before dinner."

"A small one please," replied Cole. Mozart filled the room as Cole accepted a glass from his host, who pulled a straight chair near Cole.

"I carefully check this room daily for monitoring devices but if somehow I miss something the music should render our quiet conversation indecipherable."

"The deception was difficult to initiate, but the seriousness of the situation motivated me to play my part before your colleagues, but misleading your wife in your home about our relationship is awkward and possibly dangerous. She may realize that we are wary of each other and have no real bond," cautioned Cole.

" I have told Anneleise that you are introverted and taciturn so that she would not be concerned about the absence of male comradery she is used to seeing with old friends," Gerbold responded.

"Does your wife know anything about your plan for leaving this privileged life behind?" asked Cole.

"No, but she will be told when she needs to know. It is safer for her that way."

"She will accept your decision?"

"She will when I explain what will happen if we stay," Gerbold replied.

"What would happen, assuming you just honored

your responsibilities? I cannot see you actually concerning yourself about the Nazis having a deadly virus".

"Anneleise's grandfather was a secular Jew who managed to get his surname charged to one that was typically Germanic. Her father was baptized Lutheran, as of course was she. The Nazis have become obsessed with racial purity. They have already begun to investigate prominent officials and notable citizens whose appearance, name or connections suggest Jewish heritage."

"This has also become a malicious way to harass an enemy. You report your suspicions, and the individual has to endure a disturbing, detailed review of their family. I am currently above suspicion, but my SS colleagues involved in this work openly brag about their progress and delight in relating the planned next steps in defining racial purity. All officers in the SS will soon have to submit documentation proving their non-Jewish heritage going back several generations. As my wife, Anneleise would also be investigated. I have enemies that could use this information to see that I come to an unpleasant end and my wife and child relegated to some meager existence. I cannot wait until Himmler or one of his flunkies demands our documentation. I need to get out of Germany before there is any chance of them becoming suspicious of my family's heritage."

"I understand your motivation now, which reassures me about your intentions in this affair, but remember you promised me information about Cartan as soon as I reached Germany. I want to see what you have," said Cole.

Gerbold rose from his chair and went to an Oriental desk where he removed an envelope, which he handed to Cole. Inside the worn envelop postmarked from Africa, Cole found a letter written in French. He scanned the handwritten page and looked at Gerbold.

"Your friend recognized Cartan and sent you this letter, but why would he believe you were interested in Cartan?" asked Cole.

"I had heard rumors that Cartan had gone to our former colony in Southwest Africa, and I asked my friend who is stationed there to be on the lookout for Cartan but not to approach him. My friend had seen Cartan with me years ago, but I know that Cartan was too damn drunk to remember him. You are not the only one who has scores to settle with Cartan. Knowing his whereabouts could be a valuable asset for trade."

" You are still a devious man, Gerbold" said Cole.

Gerbold sighed ," A devious man is required for this place and time. Come let us join Anneleise and Ilse for our meal."

After dinner, the two men walked down to the lake at the rear of Gerbold's property. The moon reflected brightly on the placid surface of the water. Cole felt the same anxiety he remembered as a young man looking out at a peaceful Gulf of Mexico knowing that within hours hurricane force winds would hurl water, trees and parts of houses at everything in its path. Only in this case, the raging wind was Himmler's SS and Gestapo, which Gerbold was daring to call forth against Cole and himself like interlopers stealing rubies from a sacred statue. Perhaps Gerbold and Cole had done enough wickedness that they deserved fiery retribution but exposing innocents, Anneleise and Ilse, to undeserved ruin was deeply troubling to Cole.

Gerbold drew Cole back towards the villa, stopping at the perimeter of a copse where two wooden lawn chairs sat side-by-side. Gerbold waved Cole to one of the lawn chairs while he reclined on the other. The wood felt cool and damp, even through Cole's clothing.

"Long distance listening devices cannot reach us here. I thought you might want to know my plan for retrieving the virus and the vaccine," said Gerbold.

"Your scientist cannot manage this? He certainly has access," asked Cole.

"He is carefully searched every time he leaves the laboratory area and finally before leaving the building. I cannot envision a way for him to remove the samples without detection."

" Are you confident that you and I can obtain the materials in the building? Are you sure this is possible? I do not volunteer for suicide missions."

"It has to be possible, your government will not help me unless they get the samples,"

"That does not reassure me. I need to believe you have a sound plan before I risk my neck," said Cole.

"Well, you are not going to like your part. Our scientist will put specially dried virus in sealed bottles along with ampules of vaccine into a small padded metal tube. The vaccine may not survive transport, but we will have a description of the process to make the vaccine as a backup. We will hide the tube in a little used storage room on the top floor of the facility . You have to scale the side of the building to enter a single window in the room, obtain the tube and descend with it back to the ground."

"I am not a climber. How, on earth, am I going to go up and down a vertical stone wall like a fly?"asked Cole incredulously.

"I doubt a normal human could make the climb quickly and noiselessly but your strength and ability to see in the near darkness make you nearly a human fly. In any event, I expect to have a rope for you to use to scale the wall. I intend that our scientist friend before he leaves late, as he often does, crack open the window and suspend a fine string connected to a rope. The night guards will not notice the string. When you are ready, a gentle pull will bring the rope down for your climb."

"Hopefully, he will have secured the end to something that will support my weight," Cole said caustically.

"We will discuss all the details later when we have more time. You are needed for this because this is a two-man job, and I cannot do the climbing," Gerbold said as he waved his gloved prosthetic hand in the air.

"What became of my hand? Besides my longing for it, I would be disturbed if you had fed it to a pig or a dog," Gerbold demanded.

"Your pistol, short sword and hand were retained as evidence. Eventually, an undertaker cremated your hand. The sword and pistol were to be sold to benefit the county, but I am pretty sure the constable kept the pistol. I specifically requested your sword and, after making a generous donation to the constable's favorite charity, I took it home where I have it in a bureau in my bedroom. The officials, who all but abducted me while I was in Washington, gave me no time to return home to retrieve it. Since your father gave it to you, I will return it to you, assuming that you avoid getting me killed while I am here."

Gerbold rose and stretched .

"Come, I am sure you are tired from your long trip. We will find another time to finish our planning. You need to be fresh for your conference tomorrow. You have to appear truly interested to uphold your cover story."

When morning came, a servant brought breakfast for Cole and said that Cole and the Baron would leave the house in half an hour. When Cole came down the stairs to the atrium, the Baron was waiting in his immaculate SS officer uniform with his face masked with a fitted balaclava and sunglasses. The effect was chilling, a sinister SS boogie man waiting to drag his victim to hell.

"You are not yet dressed for the day," the Baron said incredulously.

" Did you forget your sun apparel in your room?"

"No, after our last contretemps, my condition greatly improved. My hat and glasses will suffice for our little excursion today," Cole replied.

The Baron glanced at his driver.

Not wanting to reveal sensitive information in front of a probable informer, he cheerily said, "Well, let's be off. We can discuss your miraculous restoration tonight."

In the car the Baron gestured at the driver. "Klaus will drop me at the Institute first then accompany you to your meeting. As you have no doubt noticed, he is wearing a business suit, not his uniform. Your colleagues might be reluctant to talk to you with an SS man as your minder. Klaus's English is less than stellar, but he will be able to interpret for you as the need arises. Your new friends will not be surprised that an important American doctor, such as yourself, has an accomplished factotum to assist him."

The Baron confined his comments for the remainder of the drive to the Institute to pointing out various landmarks along the route. In spite of his studied good spirits, Cole could tell that the Baron was agitated by Cole's recovery. His curiosity about Cole's new state was palpable. Cole surmised that the Baron was also anxious about the possibility that Cole no longer had the strength and abilities that were essential to the successful breach of the research facility.

Once the Baron had left the car, Klaus began to ask Cole about himself and the conference Cole was attending. Cole cautiously answered his questions and pivoted the conversation back to Klaus himself.

"How long have you worked with the Baron, Klaus?"

"Since the Baron became associate director of the Institute a year ago. He has had to work hard to make the Institute respond to the Führer's demands for accountability. These scientists were happy to please themselves with their pet projects and take the Reich's money without consideration of the Führer's objectives, " sniffed Klaus.

"Things are different now. The director is very intelligent and a respected scientist, but he needed the strong hand of the military and the party to remove the non-German element that could not be trusted and redirect the research for the Reich's real needs."

"Non-German element? I would have thought that a sensitive research facility such as yours would have always exclusively employed German citizens."

"All, German citizens yes, true Germans, pure German Aryan stock, unfortunately no. Quite a few had to leave. The director is too soft. He initially claimed the Institute would suffer greatly from the loss of so many scientists but the Baron was able to show him how these individuals were like parasites, sucking out valuable resources, sabotaging hard-working, true German scientists and casting a negative, gloomy pall over the prospects for the successful implementation of the new objectives of the Institute."

"What happened to all of these terminated scientists?" asked Cole.

" They went home. This is the new Germany. There is no place here for non-Aryan workers in our society. The party has made their position clear. They can work among their own people or leave the country, but they will not displace good Germans anymore."

Cole had more questions for Klaus, but with their arrival at the conference site, he deferred them for his next solo ride with Klaus. Klaus deftly located the conference organizer and introduced Cole. Prof. Muller effusively welcomed his distinguished American colleague and saw that Cole was introduced to the other organizers of the conference and to the principal speakers. Most of the key attendees spoke English, albeit haltingly in many instances. Cole's dilemma was that all the speakers would be presenting in their native German. Fortunately, a printed collection of the speaker's papers was available for the conference participants. Cole had developed a reasonable ability to read scientific and medical German over the years and thought that he could keep up with the scheduled program.

He chose a seat against the wall in the back of the room to avoid disturbing the gathering when he wanted Klaus to translate for him. Cole assuaged his embarrassment at being at a learned society meeting without command of the host language by reminding himself that he was only here as a cover for his real mission and that he would not likely suffer professionally if this assemblage collectively thought him to be an arrogant dilettante.

The morning session went well enough since Cole was familiar with all the topics comprising this portion of the schedule. At a luncheon for the attendees, he participated in an interesting discussion of the favorite treatments for schizophrenia in German-speaking countries compared to the United States. Cole could not completely suppress his discomfort at the number of physicians who were convinced that schizophrenia was inherited and favored sterilization of all patients with that diagnosis. Cole's skepticism regarding doctors Klaxon and Ruden's research suggesting schizophrenia was transmitted by a recessive gene was viewed as childish denial of the scientific evidence.

Professor Muller soon engaged Cole in a lengthy discussion of the medical community in East Tennessee, which was sufficiently boring to their table mates that everyone left the table to Cole and Muller before the afternoon session commenced. Even Klaus excused himself for a trip outside for a smoke.

As soon as they were alone, Muller said,"My colleagues believe you are here to spy on them for the new regime. Having the muscular young Klaus as your guard dog is adding to their paranoia. They want to be on record as supporting a genetic basis for schizophrenia since Hitler's people want to discredit a psychological basis for the disease, which they view as Jewish nonsense perpetrated by Freud's disciples.

"There are economic factors at work as well. Our asylums have dramatically filled with schizophrenics in the last 20 years, to the point of leaving insufficient beds for other patients. If you convince everyone that schizophrenics are hopeless and, as Hoche and Binding proposed in 1922, are life unworthy creatures then you can demand extermination of these burdens to society. Many of my colleagues share these views as part of their overall acceptance of eugenics, but many, who do not, are afraid to publicly voice their opposition because of the current political climate. I am appalled by this loss of humanitarian ideals, but I accept that I cannot change the path that has been chosen. I do not deny being a coward, but I am most concerned for my family, should I be seen as an obstacle to the fulfillment of the Reich's plans. "

Cole was shocked by Mueller's candor.

"How can you be sure that I'm not reporting on you and some of the others at this meeting?"

Mueller smiled .

"I have spent a lifetime studying my fellow man. In spite of your efforts to avoid revealing your revulsion at my colleagues views, your true feelings were obvious to me."

"Well, now it is my turn to be trusting, but all I can tell you is that I am here to help an old acquaintance," replied Cole.

Mueller paused before responding ,

"This is not the grand Germany of my youth. There is much talk about restoring order and the rule of law, but these are dangerous times, and the law is just what these ruthless men say that it is. I will not talk to you again privately, that could be dangerous for both of us. Good luck to you, young man."

At the end of the day, Cole was emotionally drained and actually happy to be back in Werner's house. A known evil bastard seemed easier to stomach that a confederation of cowards so paralyzed by fear that their morality was calcified and a willingness to betray colleagues was assumed. Werner was still out but Anneleise entertained Cole in the great room over-looking the lake at the rear of the house. The expanse of floor to ceiling glass made the lake look like an extension of the house. Anneleise let Cole admire the view as the sun gave its final performance of the day highlighting the charms of the rippling waves being blown about by a mischievous evening wind. She finally insisted that he sit and served him hors d'oeuvres and a nice Reisling.

" I admit I feel a little melancholic. This wonderful view, the comfort of your home, good wine and a stunningly beautiful hostess. I reluctantly envy Werner. I cannot imagine actually having a real family. I have denied myself for so many years because of my circumstances that I rarely think about what I'm missing," Cole confessed.

" You surprise me, Cole . I would never have guessed that you were so alone."

" Self-imposed. You know that Werner and I are set apart. Beyond our unusual diet, we do not age as fast as others. That has always been a stumbling block for me. Seeing Werner succeed in having a family with a loving daughter is liberating for me."

Anneleise smiled ,"Ilse is certainly not your usual little girl, more a little minx, but I understand your meaning, yes, she is a perfectly normal human being. As time passes maybe Werner and I will meet somewhere in the middle as we age, but I can see the effect of time on Werner. You, on the other hand, I doubt you look all that different from the young surgeon who went to war over 15 years ago. I can see how that would be a problem in a long-term relationship. Since we are alone, I need to ask some hard questions of you. I can see that you and Werner are not old friends, more probably old rivals or antagonists.. So why are you here?" asked Anneleise.

"I was asked to help Werner, for what purpose I cannot tell you. I had no real choice in the matter, but as a sweetener, Werner gave me the location of a man who probably killed my fiancé over 10 years ago. The day will come when I will force that man to tell me the truth about her death."

" So another reason to avoid relationships, the violent loss of a true love . I better understand that faint aura of sadness that follows you, Cole. Is what you do for Werner dangerous?" asked Anneleise.

"Werner has every incentive to see that I am as safe as a baby in his mother's arms." replied Cole.

Anneleise considered Cole's statement.

"If Werner is completely invested in your safety that suggests that we all are at risk. I hope Werner knows what he is doing. He works with very dangerous people. They can appear warm, friendly, companionable, but they are basically thugs, they will do anything to get what they want."

Anneleise rose from the sofa on hearing Werner come into the house.

"Please stay seated, Cole."

Werner soon entered the room, his face pale and strained. He sat in a chair near Cole, speaking in a low voice.

"My superior has taken an interest in your presence in Germany. I underestimated his paranoia and attention to detail. Since you will never set foot in my Institute, I did not think he would be curious about you as my house guest," said Werner.

"You hoped he would not. He probably had no problem identifying me as a former Army officer, and you would know better than I what sort of links exist between our names in Interpol reports. This scrutiny may end up scuppering our little break-in excursion,

" Cole said icily.

"We have to complete the project. You know why," Werner said barely above a whisper.

Cole wanted to yell and stomp out of the room, but he now reluctantly shared the obligation to shelter Anneleise and Ilse.

Before Cole could say anything else, Werner continued, "We have to attend a party tonight. Fuchs has indicated that he would like to meet you and, as it happens, he has an invitation to a reception at the American Embassy. We are to meet him there."

"God in Heaven," said Cole.

"Yes , Gott im Himmel," echoed Werner.

"Do you think your boss, this Fuchs, wants to see if the American military attaché gives us away by reacting to our unexpected presence?"

"I have met the attaché before so if he does not have a good poker face, seeing us together could be a shock for him. Hopefully, he has not seen your photograph and will not immediately realize the implications of our joint attendance. Fuchs will make a point of seeing that you are introduced, but I suspect the attaché will subdue his visceral reaction and will just politely interact with you as an American guest of his German friends and colleagues," Werner responded.

"When do we leave?"

"As soon as I change my uniform."

Werner said little as he and Cole were driven to the current temporary embassy location in the Tiergarten area on Benderstrasse. He told Cole that the Blucher Palace was to be the permanent home of the embassy, but a fire damaged that location and repairing the damaged building had been a slow process, especially because of the soured politics once the Nazis had taken over the government . American Embassy receptions were popular, and the building was packed with attendees from other embassies and a wide range of German officials.

Werner skillfully navigated through the throngs with Cole in close attendance. Periodically, Werner stopped and introduced Cole to embassy officials of old acquaintance. Early on in their slog through the crowd, Cole realized that Werner's irregular path was centered on a line aiming at the far side of the reception room where a uniformed SS officer was watching their approach with interest.

"Standartenfuhrer , may I present Dr. Cole Sterling, my honored guest, "Werner said when they reached the officer's side.

" Cole, this is Standartenfuhrer Fuchs. He was kind enough to see that we were included under his invitation to the reception tonight."

"Thank you for arranging for our presence here. For an American citizen, it is eye-opening to actually see our embassy at work in Berlin. My stay in Berlin is sadly all too brief. I did not expect to have the good fortune to see our embassy and certainly not to participate in a diplomatic reception here," said Cole, hoping that he did not sound too sycophantic.

"Werner tells me that you are attending a psychiatric meeting in Berlin. Do we treat mental illness differently than the United States?" inquired Fuchs .

"The world of science and medicine is closely connected between Europe and the United States. We have similar approaches, but there are differences in favored treatments. Doctors tend to utilize the methods favored by their teachers and mentors. That sometimes leads to regional differences in therapy for a particular disease, at least for a while. The scientific method eventually sorts these things out."replied Cole.

"Military science has similar biases. War colleges can turn out officers who think too alike because of too much deference to the views of old vaunted generals. Fortunately, our Fuhrer is enlightened and realizes that future military actions cannot be updated versions of old strategies. We must have a complete break with the past, new thinking, new leaders. Germany cannot accept a stalemate, a humiliation, such as occurred in the last war."

"In America and in England , the last war was called the war to end all wars. I had hoped that might be true," said Cole quietly.

Fuchs body stiffened and his eyes narrowed . " I think you understand our history after the war. My people have endured a great injustice. We are required to right many wrongs. Our Fuhrer will demand these inequities be redressed. If his demands are met, military conflict can be avoided, but stubborn resistance to honoring just claims for restitution will have severe consequences."

The French ambassador, fortuitously, approached Werner and Fuchs before Fuchs could expand his diatribe. He gregariously greeted them and invited them to a full moon Boar hunt he was organizing for next month. The ambassador , who was a little tipsy, had been aggressively strong-arming the younger, fitter men to ensure that he had a large party for this adventure. It was at this point that the American military attaché joined their little group. The tall, smiling attaché had chosen to wear a well-cut suit instead of his military uniform.

" I hear Monsieur Pelletier has stealthily subverted our reception to secure companions for his escapade chasing poor little pigs around in the night. Gerbold and Fuchs, I hope you have not been corralled into Monsieur Pelletier's wild enterprise. "

The attaché looked quizzically at Cole while Monsieur Pelletier enlarged on the healthy benefits of chasing wild boar with him and his friends.

"I do believe we have not met. I am Major Jordan Thomas, military attaché here in Berlin."

"Cole Sterling, I am briefly visiting with my old friend Werner Gerbold and have the good fortune to be in attendance at your wonderful reception."

"An American, good Lord, you are a long way from home. Where do you hale from in the states?" asked Thomas.

"East Tennessee," said Cole.

"Well I'll be, my wife is from Chattanooga. If you are

here for long, she will want to meet you. Well, I will leave you to my good buddies Gerbold, Fuchs and Pelletier. My ambassador is not happy if I do not keep on circulating. I hope you enjoy your visit."

"I have to visit with some of the attendees, myself, before I leave. A pleasure to meet you Dr. Sterling,"said Fuchs.

"The pleasure is all mine, Standartenfuhrer," replied Cole.

Fuchs set out for his quarry but stopped abruptly, pivoted and stared at Cole momentarily before turning away.

"He recognizes me now."

"What do you mean?

" That's the sonofabitch that overran my field hospital and shot me, very deliberately, while I was lying helplessly on the ground after being bayoneted by one of his troops."

Werner's pale complexion now resembled ivory.

He gasped, "Fuchs will scrutinize every aspect of our relationship. He will increase our surveillance from routine to active threat evaluation."

Cole could see Werner forcing himself to remain outwardly calm.

"I will introduce you to the American ambassador on our way out. We should go." stammered Werner.

Werner nervously accelerated preparation for extraction of the samples before the cold hand of Fuchs tore them away to a horrible death. Werner briefed Cole on his plan for removing the virus from the laboratory. He spoke of these things only for a few minutes at a time in locations around the outside of his house that he believed were surveillance free.

On Sunday, Werner announced that they were going into the forest to look for mushrooms. They were to appear to accidentally meet the defecting scientist while collecting some fine specimens for their dinner. Their scientist was a well-known mushroom hunter in the summer and fall and often spent his Sundays in the forest. Herr Koch insisted on meeting Cole to assuage his fear that Werner was duping him into fully incriminating himself before arresting him. Koch was to prove himself to Cole and Werner by providing a recipe for cultivating the virus and a summary of the steps essential to preparing a vaccine. Cole would secure the virus and vaccine immediately before they all left Germany by plane.

There were several forests at the edges of Berlin where they could hope to find mushrooms, but these would be crowded with hikers, picnickers, and competing mushroomers. Werner drove further to ensure a less crowded venue for their meeting. In the event that they were followed, a quieter setting gave him a reasonable chance of spotting Fuchs' nosy underlings before they came too close to their threesome.

Werner and Koch had agreed to meet on a particular trail near a small lake. Koch would lead them off the trail to look for auspicious trees and ground disturbances where he hoped to find his prey. Koch intended to talk while they picked the desired Marone, Steinpilze, or Pfifferlinge. The surrounding forest was pleasant and the trail Cole and Werner followed was challenging enough that Cole had to concentrate on his footing, mitigating his obsessing on the danger inherent in this meeting. They had a great cover story, but Fuchs would never believe that the three men were innocently picking mushrooms.

Koch waited at the bend in the trail at the edge of the lake. He was a tall, thin, fidgety man in his 50s. Cole suspected his restless movements were part of his constitution, not a sign of nervousness, but they were an unfortunate characteristic for a traitor. An observer watching them from a distance would easily believe that Koch was a nervous, cowardly degenerate exposing state secrets. All the more reason to pray that Fuchs men were nowhere about. Koch and Cole greeted each other perfunctorily. Everyone wanted to escape into the sheltering woods with minimal delay.

Koch abruptly bounded uphill into dense foliage with Cole and Werner dodging shrubs and trees as they scampered along behind his retreating figure. Away from the lake, the ground cover was less dense and Cole and Werner were able to stride normally to stay apace with Koch. The canopy of leaves permitted a muted, serene light to bathe the forest floor. Cole was surprised how quickly Koch found a cluster of Marone, which he quickly placed in his and Werner's collection baskets. Koch seemed to relax once they had secured choice edibles to validate the innocence of their excursion. He rattled on about recognizing the mushrooms morphology and suggested ways to use them in tasty dishes. Cole realized that Koch hoped that he and Werner would recall his lessons if they should be interrogated by any of Fuchs' goons.

Near the top of the hill, where they seemed safe from scrutiny for a while, Koch stared intensely at Cole, scanning him carefully for the first time.

"Can you really recover the viral specimens and the vaccine from the Institute?" He asked.

"If you and Werner have it near the window in the storage room as planned, I will retrieve it,"replied Cole.

"And you, Baron, are you certain the plane will be in place for us after you have the virus?"

" I assure you that no one is readier to leave Germany than me . The plane will be there for us."

"Have you familiarized yourself with the marsh where we are to meet, Herr Koch?" continued Werner.

" Yes, I found the elevated access road at the edge of the marsh just as you described it. But it does not go far at all, it ends at the edge of the marsh. Where will a plane land?"

"The other side of that end of the marsh elevates and there is a narrow strip of fallow fields before the forest picks up again. A small plane can land there to retrieve us. We have to leave our cars at the access road and walk through the marsh to get to the other side but the passage is narrow there, only a little over a kilometer. The marsh is nearly dry now and we will get across easily . The plane will land just before dark, but the pilot can take off in the dark if he has to. The pilot knows his business," Werner assured Koch.

"When do we leave?" Koch asked.

"When I do my next inspection of your laboratory, you can slip the container into my coat pocket. The guards search all of you leaving the room, but they are perfunctory in their scrutiny of me. After all, I am their boss. When I am out of the laboratory, I will pretend to inspect the storage room on your floor and hide the container near the window where Cole will enter for the retrieval."

"I am concerned about the virus maintaining viability during transport and will have several samples processed in different ways to improve our chances of having something for our efforts."

"I trust you Herr Koch, if anyone can succeed at this I know you can. Of course if we don't end up with viable organism, we have your documentation, which is still valuable. You should know, Herr Koch, that my boss, Fuchs, has realized that Cole is an odd and suspicious companion. I suspect that he will be at the Institute this week, maybe even Monday, to look around. Should this occur ,hopefully ,we can turn this to our advantage. The guards will not search him or me if we are inspecting your lab together. If you have a safe opportunity to put the container in my pocket, do so. I will get into the storage room after Fuchs is gone."

Koch stared at Werner wide-eyed.

"I am not a soldier like you, Baron. To do this thing in front of a man who would torture and kill us if he discovers the transfer is very frightening. I do not know that I can summon the courage for this," stammered Koch.

"You must. We are both committed at this point. We have to leave Germany. Fuchs would never suspect that we would be so brazen as to do this under his nose. Remember, although he is suspicious of me, he has no evidence of my disloyalty and no idea of what my goals might be if I were disloyal."

Koch looked back and forth at Cole's and Werner's faces, looking for the strength and reassurance he sorely needed at this juncture. He looked away with resignation.

"I hope you truly know what you are doing, and I hope I have the courage to do my part," Koch said forlornly.

Werner clapped Koch on the shoulder. "Come, Herr Koch, let us go home. As you can see , I am burning up in this coat."

Werner had not worn a balaclava for their excursion today but was otherwise completely covered. His face was smeared with a heavy coating of zinc oxide, which gave him a ghastly sheen around his sunglasses, as he perspired copiously. The three men trudged back down the hill, parting at the trail to return to their vehicles. Koch and Werner had parked at opposite ends of the trail so that their automobiles would not be seen in proximity. Werner hoped that Fuchs' goons were too lazy to check both areas.

"You drive, I am getting in the back,"ordered Werner.

"Don't you think seeing me at the wheel is an invitation for Fuchs people to pull us over ?" Cole asked incredulously.

" I am an SS officer. If I say it is my order that you drive me, it is, by definition, correct behavior, and I will shoot them if they argue."

Werner climbed in the back seat, muttering and swearing, while loosening his coat. His face looked even ghastlier that it had when they were with Koch. Cole could see there was no appealing to reason with Werner. He got in the massive vehicle and prayed he could drive it well enough to avoid wrecking them or attracting a police vehicle. The automobile lurched several times as Cole worked the gears but settled into a smooth run along the road back to Werner's home . Werner began to sing a German folk song that Cole had heard somewhere, but before Cole could ask about it, Werner abruptly asked, "Why are you still unmarried? You have those two beautiful sisters to choose from and you do not select one. You can see how I have benefited from being married, that is what keeps me away from my darker impulses."

Cole steelily enunciated, "Werner you abducted and abused one of those women and threatened the other. You are not someone who should be casually inquiring about them or my relationship with them. I see that you are attempting to walk a different path, and I am trying to help your family, in spite of our past history, but I should not have to listen to this."

" Cole, I have many informants. I know that Catherine took over the running of her father's factory, and Clover is a fashion designer in New York. Both successful, strong women, but there is a reason neither has married. You need to decide. Pick one. Maybe then the other will move on."

Werner's voice was fading out as he pontificated.

"I don't feel well, I think I will take a little nap."

Cole glanced over his shoulder. Werner was not perspiring as profusely but his face now looked flushed under the zinc oxide. His closed eyes looked sunken and pale against the ruddy background of his face.

"Damn, damn, damn" Cole muttered and drove faster, watching his mirrors and swiveling his head to look for lurking police.

After what seemed an eternity, he brought the vehicle into Werner's driveway too fast and swerving. He hopped out and hollered for one of the servants. In short order, a butler emerged followed closely by Anneliese.

"Strip him and get him into a cold bath immediately. He is going from heat exhaustion into heatstroke. Get all the ice you can find," ordered Cole.

Cole and the butler struggled to lift Werner, basically manhandling him into the bathtub, which Anneliese had filled with cold water.

"Is he going to be all right?" asked Anneliese anxiously.

"It would be tough going for most people, but he is stronger than most and should come around quickly," replied Cole.

Werner had cursed and jerked as he received the full impact of the cold water. He fought for a while before resting against the back of the tub. The maid appeared soon outside the bathroom door with a bucket of large ice fragments from a block of ice from the ice box . Werner was adapted enough to the cold water that he only muttered as they placed the ice in the water.

"Anneliese, we need a thermometer to monitor his temperature," said Cole.

When she returned with the thermometer, Cole put it under Werner's tongue and had the butler hold it, while grasping and steadying his jaw.

"He could seize. We don't want him to crush the thermometer in his mouth."

"He does not look as red," said Anneliese. Cole removed the thermometer.

"He is down to 39.2°C that is a good start. He was probably above 40° earlier."

Cole took Werner's temperature several times and noticed Werner's increased shivering.

"We are at 38°. Let's get him out and get him into bed."

They carefully removed Werner from the water, pat dried him and maneuvered him into bed where they covered him with a thin sheet. He continued to shiver, but he looked better and had begun to talk to Anneliese.

"When he is a little better offer him mineral water, but sips only. Later add a little salt to replace what he lost earlier with his heavy perspiration. Watch him carefully. Let me know if you need me," said Cole.

Cole retreated to Werner's study where he secured a scotch from the antique sideboard where Werner kept a few bottles ready to hand. The maid had stocked the ice bucket with crushed ice, which Cole delighted in as he dropped some into his glass. He collapsed into a well -padded club chair and attempted to stop ruminating on the mounting disaster he perceived in this awful situation into which he had been hijacked.

Anneliese entered the study with evidence of recent tears. She waved her hand to keep Cole from rising and sat near him with an air of exhaustion.

"I took the liberty of pouring myself a strong one. May I prepare you a drink?" Cole asked.

"No , I will have one later, when I calm down. I know something is wrong. I know Werner and I know that he has been on edge for some time awaiting your arrival. He must have brought you here to do something very dangerous."

Cole got up and kneeled next to Anneliese. "Werner would not want us talking where someone could hear us or record us, so I will whisper. You are correct. I am here to help with something very important and we have very little time. Hopefully, Werner will bounce back right away. Werner will confide in you , I promise. We will do everything possible to protect you and Ilse."

Anneleise stared at Cole for several seconds before looking away and saying in a low voice, "I will try my best to be patient and strong, but I cannot hold up without knowing everything as soon as he is better. I definitely want that drink now."

The next morning , Werner, on cursory examination, looked his usual self, but it was clear to Cole that he was struggling to not show his fatigue.

" We will go together today. I will drop you off at the conference. Is it today or tomorrow that is the last day?"

"Tomorrow, but it is just morning sessions before adjournment."

"I gave the driver off today so I will be driving," stated Werner.

In the car Werner said, "We will go tonight. The scrutiny will only get worse. We cannot afford to wait".

"Can you arrange our escape on short notice?"

"Yes, I would have wanted to proceed soon anyway, but with the new circumstances, we will set everything in motion immediately. Any delay could be catastrophic. I will hide the specimens today once I alert Koch to assembly everything in the travel tube."

The men completed the remainder of their drive together silently, each pondering his own thoughts. Cole knew there were too many parts to this mission, each of which had to work perfectly to lead to the desired happy ending, a ride off into the sunset finale that they all wanted. The overall complexity strained credulity to assume that they would succeed and escape to safety.

Werner ruminated on the wraith he would bring down on his wife and daughter if they failed. He struggled to maintain his resolve and suppress the haunting voices taunting him that his family would suffer total destruction as punishment for his history of cruelty and lack of compassion for the many tortured souls that he had used and manipulated for his personal gratification and need for dominance.

Exalted beings, due to their intellectual, physical and genetic superiority deserved submission from the masses, who should be honored to be used by these endowed individuals. This had been his personal mantra since he was a young man and had been a factor in his attraction to Nazism. How wondrous that his inner knowledge of superiority was now endorsed by a new political movement, who supported him in his visions of personal grandeur.

With the birth of Ilse and the continued exposure to his wife's religious devotion to a loving God who expected personal humility, Werner began to realize that he was on the wrong side of his relationship with God and, no doubt, with the judgment of history as well. He fervently hoped, prayed, that his awful arrogance and sins of the past would not doom his beloved wife and child.

The somber men merely nodded silently at each other as Cole left the vehicle on this day that would begin the countdown to either the successful culmination of their task or catastrophic downfall.

Werner tried after they parted to redirect his thoughts to the prosaic minutia of his workday and view those details with calculation to identify opportunities to ensure that the handoff was well executed and the travel tube well hidden in the storage room . He had not been in that room in a few weeks, and he hoped that nothing significant had changed from his last exploration of its recesses.

By the time he reached the Institute, he had regained much of his confidence and managed to look the part of a carefree, powerful director of an important Institute of the Reich. Werner sent an innocuous short memo to the laboratory staff in Koch's lab, which, by prior agreement, would alert Koch that today was the day for the stealthy transfer of the travel tube. Having initiated the process, he relaxed and worked his way through the piles of paperwork required to address the scientific and bureaucratic demands of the Institute. Late morning, his secretary announced that Standartenfuhrer Fuchs was in the outer office and required him to accompany him for a surprise inspection of the facility.

Werner smiled and thought you are right on schedule to play your part in achieving our goal. After donning his jacket, Werner greeted Fuchs in the outer office.

"Standartenfuhrer, what a pleasure. A surprise, but a pleasant one, since I have the honor of your company. Shall we talk first in my office or do you want to begin your inspection immediately?"asked Werner.

He intentionally would act agreeable to any approach that Fuchs might prefer. He knew that men such as Fuchs made a point of throwing you off balance. If you wanted to suggest a way to conduct a review, they regarded that as suspicious. Best to let them have a free hand and satisfy any of their demands and answer any of their questions, no matter how inane.

"Let us begin. I have other activities today and since I also intend to be thorough, we should be efficient with our time."

"Of course, do you have a specific order for your tour?"

"Yes, I will see all the laboratories in order from the first floor to the top, and I want to see all the storage areas along the way.Are the most dangerous samples contained on the fifth floor?"

"Yes, we are considering moving them to the basement where we may create better safety measures in the event of accidents, but there is a lot of expensive work to be done before that can occur, and the plans are not finalized. You will, of course, receive detailed descriptions for your approval when we have finished the evaluation."

They went from lab to lab without prior warning, although those labs that had telephones no doubt had been alerted. There were no phones in Koch's laboratory. However, since it would take time for them to reach the top floor, Werner surmised that Koch would be forewarned. Werner was concerned that, in spite of Werner's warning that Fuchs might arrived today, this intelligent, but slightly neurotic, scientist would expose them with his nervous demeanor. Werner could readily envision Koch, having dwelled on Fuchs presumed suspicions all night, being in such an agitated state that he had convinced himself that Fuchs was here today to confront, accuse and arrest them.

Werner worried that Koch might confess if Fuchs simply aggressively questioned him about routine security for the dangerous organism that was his primary responsibility. Werner silently prayed, a practice he had only recently begun to explore, but considering his past , he did not feel confident that his prayers attracted any attention from the Almighty. Nauseated and weak, Werner struggled to maintain his composure with Fuchs as they moved from laboratory to laboratory. Werner also knew he had to manage the inspection in such a way that his staff felt appropriately protected from this visiting ogre and not, in any way ,feel that their assistant director had lost control of the situation.

Werner was actually relieved by the time they reached the fifth floor. Fuchs had been attentive to Werner's presentation of the duties of each laboratory and had made notes as they proceeded. Up to now, other than the timing, this seemed like a normal inspection. Koch's laboratory was the last on the list, appropriately so, since this laboratory worked with the most dangerous specimens. The laboratory was quite large because the work areas were separated for safety and at one end of the room was a specially designed area for storage of the many virulent specimens in their collection. Werner was pleased to see the small staff in this room wearing their mandated safety equipment and apparently working normally on their experiments. Werner and Fuchs donned protective equipment just outside of the entrance before beginning their review. Werner began a slow walk around the perimeter of the room with the intention of leaving Koch's station for last.

Fuchs asked many questions about the equipment, safety provisions, medical hazards and the goals of the experimentation with each organism at the various work stations. Just as they were approaching Koch, Fuchs opined,

"Given how deadly these organisms are, I do not see how they could ever be used in biological warfare without also killing our troops."

"As you have seen, we have many experiments to better understand how the organisms function to kill or disable and how easily we can decontaminate a large area that has been disseminated with the agent. Knowledge really is power. We might have to protect ourselves from biologic attack, and if we choose to use a specific agent against the enemy, we have to anticipate exactly the area it will affect and how to contain the agent. Most agents will not be useful to us at our current level of understanding, but we do have a short list that in special circumstances could be deployed,"Werner answered before quickly moving on to Koch before Fuchs could ask for more details.

"Herr Koch is one of our senior scientists and devotes most of his time to a very virulent blistering virus that quickly leads to death. Currently, this agent would be of value only in a strategic attack intended to decimate a large population, but even to use it in that fashion would require a vaccine to protect our occupying troops after the virus has subdued the enemy."

Fuchs sniffed," Our best strategists would rather quickly overrun a population and then utilize them to run their economy for our benefit. Although perhaps, a biological agent such as you described might be valuable in cleansing a broad area of masses possibly too intractable to be of much value to us. Jews and Communists in those parts of Russia where we would not be welcomed as saviors comes to mind."

"How far along are you with the vaccine?" Fuchs asked Koch.

Koch replied, without nervousness," I am close, but there is much testing to be done before I am ready for human trials. The animal studies are promising so far."

"I want you to immediately start human trials. We may need this agent and a vaccine very soon. I will order that suitable test subjects be provided. You will start next week."

"As you wish, Standartenfuhrer, " responded Koch.

Fuchs turned from Koch and took a final long look around the large room. Werner had also turned away as Fuchs collected his final impressions. Werner was startled to feel the travel tube slid into his jacket pocket as Koch managed to move his hand around the protective gown.. Werner did not look back at Koch. He followed Fuchs back to the entrance of the room where they removed goggles, masks and gowns . Werner glanced at his jacket pocket to ensure that the tube did not project. The bulge was somewhat notable, but hopefully Fuchs would not notice the difference.

As they approached the only elevator that reached this floor, Fuchs paused and said "I nearly forgot. We are not finished until I see the storage room on this floor. "

"Certainly, Standartenfuhrer. This way."

The little room was a little dusty but neatly arranged.

"They only store nonhazardous, non-fragile supplies here. They mostly have assistants bring what they need from other more appropriate storage areas," said Werner.

While Fuchs craned his neck to look at items on tall shelving on one side of the room, Werner quickly placed the travel tube into a preselected hiding spot . He was at Fuchs' side as Fuchs exited the room.

As they entered the elevator, Werner said, "Is there anything else I can show you today, Standartenfuhrer? I apologize that the Director is not here today to greet you. He is meeting with some of our material suppliers about changing specifications."

" I would think that would be your job," noted Fuchs.

"You are correct, but the Director is an old friend of one of the men. His friend is ill and the Director wants to see if he can be of assistance in arranging expedited medical care."

"Most thoughtful of him but hopefully not at the expense of maximum productivity here at the Institute."

"Not at all, his friend has gone to great links to see that we receive high purity chemicals, with custom specifications, for our research. It is in everyone's interest to ensure the health of such a key source, who by the way is a party member."

" I understand completely. We have to look out for our valuable colleagues." agreed Fuchs .

"Regrettably ,I have to leave now for my next appointment, I'm already late. I shall want to meet soon with the Director and you to discuss your current status on all projects and to decide on new priorities based on the latest directive from the Führer's office. Heil Hitler."

Werner lowered his hand slowly from returning Fuchs' salute as he watched Fuchs exit the front entrance. He stood quietly as he pondered the successful retrieval and concealment of the samples in the presence of their enemy. The feat was nearly incomprehensible. He had seriously underestimated the steel in Koch's spine. Werner could not afford to communicate with Koch now. They all had to trust each other to go forward from here. Werner returned to his office, where he managed to do the most essential tasks to avoid any concerns about his behavior today. As best as he could, he mulled over the requirements for the extraction of the tube from the storage room.

Werner had arranged for Klaus to pick up Cole. He drove himself home and did his best to act his usual self before and during dinner, not an easy task. Cole did the same and, fortunately for both men, Ilse attracted much attention this evening with her constant chattering and flitting from subject to subject, interspersed with many questions, the answers to which she rarely listened to for more than a few seconds. Eventually, Anneliese insisted that Ilse go up to bathe and prepare for bed, leaving the two men to their brandies.

Werner recommended that they take a walk and they went directly to the lawn chairs so they could talk freely. Werner described the events of Fuchs's visit to a wide-eyed Cole, who shook his head in wonder.

"Those are the good developments, but the unfortunate part is that we need to remove the tube tonight. We dare not wait. Fuchs was there today to see if he could ascertain what might be of special interest to the American government. He probably believes you are their agent and that they want a specific item. His visit today gave him plenty of likely targets. As we both know, he is probably getting all the information that he can about you. He will not take any chances. Once he has sufficient information to present to his superiors, he will take action. We will have to obtain the tube tonight and leave tomorrow night by plane. On my way home, I sent the message to signal for our extraction."

" Good Lord, Werner, this is sudden. You have to prepare Anneliese. I hope you have a secure way for her to get the plane, "said Cole.

" Long prepared. They will be retrieved first, and then we will be picked up at the marsh along with Koch. Our immediate problem is that Koch did not let down the string for the rope. No doubt he was waiting until I told him it was time, which I could not chance this afternoon."

"Then what am I going to do to get up the wall ."

" You will have a rope . You will see soon enough. I need to get back to prepare Anneliese. Meet me in my study of 11. I have dark clothing and darkening for our faces. We will drive over in a car not familiar to the Institute staff. There should be good cloud coverage tonight and visibility will be poor for the guards. The lighting around the Institute is subdued. I suspect Fuchs will have correcting that listed in his memorandum regarding essential security improvements. Around 1130 is a good time for our approach , since the guards change at midnight and a perimeter patrol will have been made about 11. I will see you to the edge of the woods close to the fifth floor window. There is a half over-grown path from where we leave the car to the spot closest to the window. I will direct you from there. Well, I must go to Anneliese now. She should have Ilse in bed by now. I have to somehow tell her our world is about change forever and that we have to leave everything behind."

Cole watched as the forlorned Werner trudged off to break his wife's heart and, no doubt, shock and scare her to her deepest core. Cole suspected that the man had never done anything more painful in his entire life. Any satisfaction Cole would have taken even a few days ago at Werner's predicament was now replaced by deep sadness knowing that Anneliese and Ilse would never feel safe again in this world.

At eleven, Cole met Werner in the study and changed into the dark clothing and special shoes for tonight's enterprise. They left the study by a side door into the garden and quietly walked through the grass to the toolshed at the edge of the property where the small vehicle they would use tonight was parked. They were far enough from the house that it was doubtful anyone would hear the small engine start up. Werner slowly drove the car on the grass without lights until he could turn out onto the road without fear of observation from the house. Werner was cautious from that point on to not attract any police attention with his driving. They quickly reached the area of the Institute and drove a short way into the wooded area adjacent to the main building. They left the car where it would not be seen and followed a slightly overgrown footpath to the edge of the woods near their target. Fatalistically, Cole had up to now asked no additional questions .Werner had a large bag in which Cole assumed Werner had the rope and some other items to use for the climb. Cole was shocked when Werner took from the bag a crossbow, which Cole recognized as having been mounted on the wall in the library.

" What the devil?" He exclaimed

" Patience, you will see ."Werner replied.

Werner attached a fine cord close to the tip of the

shaft of a metal arrow. This particular arrow had a savage looking arrowhead for its business end. Werner clipped the ends of the dangling cords so they would not separate and fall from the arrow while in flight. With Cole's help they managed to cock the heavy bow. Werner next withdrew from the bag a telescoping tripod to which he attached the crossbow. After careful sighting of his target, Werner released the bolt, which flew well and struck the wide apron of the fifth floor windowsill with a resounding thud.

Cole whistled," damn you are good with that thing".

"A hobby of mine and ,fortunately, I also spent two years studying engineering. Your weight will not deflect the shaft close to where it rammed into that fine old hardwood. Use the cord to pull the rope through the eye hook. Attach the clips to the rope and start working your way up the wall. Those cleated shoes will give you purchase and with your strength you should have no trouble getting up to the window. The window has been manipulated to not completely close. Take this knife in case you need to use the blade to force open the window."

Abruptly, Werner said, "Go, you don't have long before the next patrol." The rapidity and skill with which Werner had performed this last maneuver had elevated Cole's confidence that they might actually succeed at this bit of snatch and grab. He darted across a short section of grass to the wall, where he grasped the cord and attached the rope, which he then drew through the large eye hook on the arrow. Once he had the rope in place, he clipped the lower segments together. He began to pull himself up the wall using the purchase provided by the cleated shoes Werner had given him to ascend the wall. Cole knew he had only about 20 minutes to go up, secure the tube and get back to Werner before the new security detail would make their first round.

At the windowsill, he realized he had a problem. The arrow had lodged in the middle and lower end of the sill's wide apron and Cole could not hold himself safely with one hand on the rope while attempting to grasp the windowsill shelf. In spite of trying several different positions , Cole could not find one that worked. He finally went back down the rope a short distance and began to swing back and forth using his feet to propel his body until at the top of each side of the arc he was near the outer edges of the windowsill shelf. At just the right moment in the swing, he plunged Werner's knife into the top of the horizontal board. His weight was now supported by the downward pressure he was applying through the knife. Cole relaxed the tension he was applying with his other hand on the rope and wrapped the rope around this hand. Cole placed both hands on the knife handle and pulled himself onto the shelf, first with his forearms and then easing his body onto the shelf. The width of the shelf, which had thwarted his climb to now, was now an advantage, a position where he could finally reach the window.

He tried pushing it up without success. Cole eased himself further onto the shelf so that he could free the knife from the wood to use it to lever the window open. After the knife blade had done its job, Cole slowly worked the window higher until he had sufficient clearance for him to work his body through the opening. By now his muscles were painfully aching and near to spasm due to the extraordinary demands of the climb. He fell onto the floor of the storage room and would have rested there for a while if the chance of discovery were not so great. Cole forced himself to get up to retrieve the tube. Even though Cole saw well in the darkness of a usual night, the dimness of the meager light from the overcast outside sky and the absence of any light inside the room left Cole unable to make out the details of the little room. He found the pen light Werner had provided and using it quickly located the box of test tubes next to several boxes of Agar. The tubes apparently were an odd size, and the box sat here gathering dust. Inside the box, the travel tube sat in plain sight for anyone to see who lifted the box cover.

Cole removed the tube, placing it in his back pocket after first removing the bolt cutters that had been stashed there. At the window, he cautiously looked around before crawling out on the shelf, closing the window and lowering himself on the rope to the crossbow bolt. He worked the bolt cutter hard before the shaft broke and fell to the ground. Cole would not chance cutting the shaft too close to the eye hook, unfortunately, leaving a length of bolt that would eventually be found but, hopefully, not for a few days. In spite of Werner's assurances that the eye hook would hold, Cole feared falling backwards into the dark watching five stories go by in rapid succession. In spite of his fears, he reached ground quickly and uneventfully. He found the fallen arrow and sat out for Werner's hiding spot .

Just as he reached him, Werner pulled him to the ground The guards were early for their first patrol and Cole had come within seconds of running out in front of them. He cautiously repositioned himself while hugging the ground to avoid their lights as they scoured the terrain around the building. Werner had already packed the bow and tripod in the bag and moved it closer to the trail to lessen the chances of the guards seeing it. The two guards moved as a team casting their lights along all the windows and the adjacent wooded area. They rarely dwelled on one area and did not discern the subtle forms lurking in the greenery or the shortened shaft projecting from the sill. Cole speculated that had the guards had more light from the moon they would have seen them or the arrow, but the dark evening had worked in favor of the burglars. As soon as the guards rounded the building, the two men retraced their steps to the car and carefully, again without lights, made their way to the road for home.

The next day, Cole again had breakfast in his room and met Werner at the door. With Klaus at the wheel, Werner made a point of discussing a number of mundane subjects with Klaus, no doubt to ensure that he did not discern a difference in behavior on this crit-ical day. Werner left them at the Institute, while Klaus accompanied Cole to the final morning session of the convention. At the conclusion of the session, Cole spoke to as many of the participants as possible, giving them his card and inviting them to visit him should their travels bring them to Tennessee. He wondered how many of the men still considered him a spy for the regime. The continued presence of the militaristic Klaus probably did not help to dissuade them of this possibility.

On their return ride from last night's retrieval, Werner told Cole that Anneliese and Ilse were leaving midday, ostensibly, to visit and stay overnight with an old friend who was ill. She would take only two, small suitcases that were consistent with her story. She would drive herself and actually go to a remote private airfield to await the plane that would first collect Ilse and her and then, at dusk, leave to retrieve Werner, Cole, and Koch at the edge of the marsh. Werner was struggling with his emotions as he related these things to Cole. He would only say that Anneliese was despondent and frightened and, with great effort, was willing herself to act as usual with Ilse.

Cole had said little. He knew the pain Werner was experiencing and did not want to make trite comments about the situation. During the morning talks, Cole had struggled to focus his thoughts, always returning to the fact that Anneliese was being asked to leave with little more than the clothing on her back. She would probably surreptitiously include wedding and birth certificates, a few key photographs, her best jewelry and a few items of importance to Ilse. The final stab in her heart would be the realization that their departure would expose her remaining family and close friends to considerable danger from the regime..

Klaus drove Cole back to Werner's house, where Cole waited anxiously for Werner's return. His mind would not be still, jumping from one what if to another as it seemed his wait for Werner was interminable. Cole chose to wait in his bedroom to prevent the house staff from observing his nervous behavior. He had explained to the maid who usually watched over his needs that he needed solitude to do some necessary reading and write some letters. When Werner finally arrived, both men carefully gave a performance of asking about each other's day and discussing noncontroversial items from today's newspaper. They were both relieved that they actually were able to find some topics that could distract them as they made an effort to outwardly appear to be having a relaxing evening together. After dinner, Werner told the butler that they were going out for the evening to have a few drinks with Werner's friends. As they drove away from Werner's house, in spite of the poignant nature of Werner's last evening at his lush home, the men were relieved to finally be on their way to a new beginning.

Werner intentionally chose a circuitous route to the marsh but still managed to be there as planned near dusk. The access road that was their meeting point was a simple dirt track over a little peninsula of higher land overlooking the marsh. There were many high-voltage electrical towers in the marsh, and the access road provided a way for workers to get nearer the towers for maintenance. Unless they used a small road at the far end of the marsh, which was frequently impassable due to flooding, there was no way to use a vehicle to approach the towers. Most of the time they drove out on the access road and then descended on one of the small paths to the marsh below on foot. Many times they had to slog through knee-high water wearing their hip-high wadders in order to reach the towers they needed to service. As Werner had told Koch , the marsh was only wet in patches now, and the trail they would use to reach the field where the plane would land was completely dry.

Werner parked where the access road met the main road. He was relieved to see Koch's car parked similarly. Werner and Cole were dressed for an informal evening out and would be leaving literally with the clothes on their back. But they had the travel tube and the envelope with Koch's documents in their possession and were content in the knowledge that leaving with these items constituted a great success. Werner had his pistol in his jacket. Cole had chosen last evening not to return Werner's knife but had kept the knife in his hands on the way home. He had found some comfort in holding it and had decided to have it with him tonight. He knew it had limited usefulness against the current enemies, who used high-powered rifles and brute force to prey on the weak and defenseless.

Part of his comfort having the knife came from his youth. 12-year-old Cole secretly received instruction on the basics of knife fighting and how to throw a knife in bad situations from an old Indian, Joe Eagle, who worked for his father. Part of Cole's pleasure in receiving instruction from Joe was the knowledge that his father would be apoplectic knowing that his callow young son was being taught these things. Because the instruction had begun as a secret, Cole maintained his silence over the years, possibly because of guilt associated with the deception of his father, who died shortly after Joe had completed his teaching. Before leaving tonight, Cole had slid the knife in its scabbard into his sock and left the clasp loose.

As Cole and Werner walked down the middle of the access road they could see Koch at the far end. They had not gone far when Cole said, "Something is wrong. I smell and hear horses. Koch's face is not right. He has been beaten." The men continued to move cautiously towards Koch.

The access road had limited shoulders on each side. They were largely barren, except for knee-high brush in spots. Where Koch stood there was a small tree to his left. Cole said, "There is someone next to the tree. We need to leave." Before they could turn back, Cole saw Koch silently say Fuchs. Just then a shot rang out and Koch slid to the ground, shot in the head.

Before the men could move, Fuchs loudly called out, "Come, gentlemen, do not resist. Your subterfuge is over. Continue towards me. I need you to carry poor Koch back to the road. Do not attempt to leave this passage. I have mounted police at the base of the drop off. You would immediately be captured. Gerbold, as a traitor, your fate is sealed but your cooperation will help your family. Dr. Sterling, let me just say I'm pleased to see you again. I will take great pleasure in finishing what I started over 15 years ago."

At Koch's body, the two men gazed at the badly beaten Koch and wondered if he had told Fuchs the details of the incoming airplane and if Fuchs already had Anneliese and Ilse in custody. As if reading their minds, Fuchs said, "No, I don't have your family, Gerbold, but I will soon. Koch told me about your planned rendezvous at your hunting cabin in Bavaria. I have men on their way there now."

"Now, pick this traitor up," commanded Fuchs.

Werner, nearest Koch's body, bent over and clumsily lifted Koch by his shoulders. Cole pretended to be bending down to reach Fuchs feet when he pirouetted and, with a snap of his wrist, forcefully tossed the knife at Fuchs chest, where the blade ripped through Fuchs tunic into his chest. The strength of Cole's throw propelled Fuchs backward to the ground. He reflexively fired a shot from his pistol as he fell. At the sound of a second shot, the police below spurred their horses up the incline. The arrogant Fuchs must have told them to only respond if there was more than one shot fired.

Cole grabbed Werner by the arm, "Come on we can do this."

As the first horse came over the top of the incline, Cole slammed the horse in the chest with his clasped fists pushing him backwards over the edge. This so startled the horse coming over the top next to the falling horse that Cole could grab his reins and pull him close enough to deliver a powerful blow to the rider's groin. As the man gasped in agony, Cole pulled him from the saddle and mounted the horse himself. Werner had been thrown off balance by Cole's pulling him by his arm to the edge of the drop off. By now he had regained his composure, drawn his pistol and was firing at the mounted police as they emerged over the ridge.

"Come on, get on back," ordered Cole. Cole reached over and pulled Werner onto the horse and sent the horse back down the steep incline in a frightening, barely controlled slide. Both men feared the horse would completely lose his footing and toss them precipitously to the bottom. Somehow the horse made it to the dried marsh where he was rewarded by Cole with kicks to his flanks to force him into a gallop down the trail towards the field where the plane would land.

The plane had no lights but Cole was sure he saw it coming in close over the trees at the field. Dusk was now rapidly being replaced with darkness, which fortunately confounded their pursuers. They were scattered and unsure of the direction the men had taken. A few of the mounted police had discerned their movements and were racing towards them, shooting as they went. Cole could hear some of the bullets whizzing by his head as he began to push the horse up the incline to the field.

As they made it over the crest of the small hill onto the field, Cole saw the plane turning around to ready for takeoff. He berated the horse to close the distance to the plane. The poor creature was scared to death and in danger of collapsing. As they neared the plane a door was opened and a man shouted at them to hurry. Cole brought Werner next to the slow moving plane where the man in the plane pulled Werner through the door. Cole then got as near as he could to the plane as the horse was becoming greatly agitated by the noise of the motor and the rushing wind from the propeller.

Just as the horse pulled away, Cole leapt towards the door, where the man grabbed his arm and held on as Cole's feet dangled near the ground as the plane picked up speed. Cole finally grasped the edge of the fuselage and was able to help his rescuer pull him to safety. The door slammed shut as the plane accelerated, finally lifting off and sailing over the closest trees by mere feet.

The police had by now reached the field and were shooting at the plane in concentrated volleys. While most of this barrage went astray, the determined police managed to strike the fuselage multiple times, to the consternation of the plane's passengers. In spite of the best efforts of their pursuers, the plane edged steadily upwards as the pilot sought to ensure that they were well above ground-based hazards. Once the pilot achieved his goal, the plane cruised toward the nearby Polish border to escape German airspace as quickly as possible.

After Cole had managed to make it inside the plane, he struggled to absorb the scene inside the small passenger compartment. As he caught his breath, he was joyously relieved to see Anneleise and Ilse hugging Werner on a bench- like, upholstered passenger seat. Then he realized something was discordant. Anneleise was holding tight to Werner with tears streaming down her cheeks. They were not tears of joy. There was blood on Werner's jacket and blood trickled down his arm. Cole ran over to them, lifted Werner's head and said, "He must have been shot as we came over the hill. Help me. I need to remove his jacket and shirt to examine his wound."

The man who had helped Cole and Werner came back from talking to the pilot.

Cole asked, "Do you have blankets? He needs to be lying down on the other seat and covered warmly."

" I think I have two but one don't smell so good."

"Get them, please, and a first aid kit , whatever you have. Hurry and what's your name?"

As he went forward the man yelled, "Homer".

" Thank you, Homer, please hurry."

Cole removed Werner's jacket and shirt and saw that the bullet had struck Werner in the right posterior shoulder, fortunately exiting the front of his shoulder. Not so fortunately, the bullet must have struck a large vessel given the amount of blood Werner had lost. The usual imperative was to stop the bleeding, ideally replace what had been lost, and repair the damage, tasks beyond their capabilities as they made their escape.

Homer returned with a thin cotton blanket and a heavy wool blanket whose odor did suggest a possible history as a horse blanket. Cole placed the cotton blanket on the other passenger seat and, with help from Homer and Anneliese, positioned Werner so that he was chest down with his face turned so that Cole could watch his breathing. They had positioned Werner so that his right arm was on the outer edge of the seat. Cole brought Werner's arm up above his head and over the arm rest for support to keep the arm in an elevated position. Homer's first aid kit was rather sparse in supplies. There was a roll of bandage that Werner placed over the open wounds and applied firm pressure to slow bleeding.

"Anneliese, please hold pressure on these bandages. I'm going to hold pressure under his arm to reduce the flow of the brachial artery to further reduce bleeding. Based on what I am seeing, I believe the bullet nicked some larger veins not an artery. Homer, when will we reach some help? Exactly where are we going?"

"Right now, we are heading at maximum cruising speed to the border into Poland, then hugging the border northward, we will swing out over the sea and head for Copenhagen."

"Is there anywhere in Poland that we can get medical attention for this man?"

"I doubt it. We will not be near any larger places, intentionally, since we are not supposed to be in Poland, and we will pretty quickly be out over the sea ."

"How long do you think it will take us to get to Copenhagen?" asked Cole.

"Not much over an hour if we are not fighting head winds."

"What happens in Copenhagen to us?" asked Anneliese.

"I don't know. My partner and I are contractors. We just deliver you. We don't know who you are, and we don't want to know."

"Can you radio the people who are paying you so we can find out if we have an alternative to get help for this man before Copenhagen?"

"We have strict orders to maintain radio silence until our approach to Copenhagen," said Homer.

" You don't want any chance of giving away our position near the German border or flying over international waters. It is too dangerous."

Cole looked closely at Werner's face, lifted his eyelids to examine his eyes, listened carefully to his breathing and felt the pulse in his neck.

"We have to do the best we can with what we have. We seem to have the bleeding mostly under control. His pulse seems thready. He needs some IV fluids, which of course we don't have . To protect him until we can get him what he truly needs, he needs to drink some blood. This won't make up for the fact that he needs to replace the volume that has been lost, but it should revive him and keep him stable until we get somewhere where he can be properly treated."

"You and Werner did not bring a flask of blood with you?" Anneliese asked.

"No, we did not think we would need blood until after we arrived at the new location . We were also concerned that if we were stopped for a minor traffic violation, having something like that with us could lead to our being detained, even if briefly, and collapse our carefully timed escape," replied Cole.

"He can have some of my blood," said Anneliese.

"What is all this talk about drinking blood? I'm not

paid to transport vampires. Is that why we had to pick you up after the sun was down?" interjected Homer.

Cole and Anneliese laughed. "You can relax Homer . It is too complicated to explain, and I'm sure the people who are paying you would not want us discussing it, but some people need to drink blood to live, but they are not the undead. Because Werner has lost blood and has a bullet wound he needs to drink some blood to help his body to heal. After he drinks even a little blood, he will do much better until we can get him the usual medical treatment for his blood loss and bullet wound," said Cole.

"Anneliese, drinking your blood would be very helpful for Werner, but my blood probably has extra potency that would benefit Werner in his current state."

"Homer, can you get a sharp knife for me and a glass?"

"You're going to have to make do with my pocket knife and a coffee mug, I am afraid"

"That will be okay. I can work with that," Cole said with a smile.

As Homer went forward for the mug, Cole turned his attention to Ilse, who was curled in the corner of the passenger seat across from the adults. She looked like she had been crying but appeared, at this point, more stunned than anything else.

"Ilse, your daddy will be fine, but he needs us to help him until we get to where we are going. I promise you we're doing our best for him."

Cole turned to Anneliese quietly asking, "What does she know about Werner and blood? Werner had made a remark to me about her seeing Werner and I drinking our blood wine mixture with meals and being told that it was just special wine for adults only. So I assume that we have to do some explaining about what I'm going to do next."

"Yes, we saw no reason , as young as she is, to try to explain something that would be difficult for adults to comprehend, and in the world we lived in could be potentially dangerous, since young children love to tell secrets."

"I will explain a little to her," said Cole to Anneliese softly.

"Ilse, I know it sounds unpleasant but at times people need blood to live. Sometimes , the doctor gives them blood in the hospital, but a few people do not need blood that way. They drink it, sort of like you need to drink milk."

"I do not like milk, but my mother makes me drink it anyway."

"That's because you are growing and your body needs milk. Your daddy has to have blood for his body. Because of his injury he really needs it right now so I'm going to give him some of mine. Mr. Homer here was kind enough to loan me his pocketknife so that I can get some of my blood and put it in the mug for your daddy to drink. I am willing to bet that he will wake up and smile at you. Now I'm going to poke myself with the little pointed blade to get the blood flowing so we can catch it in the mug and then let your daddy start taking sips of it. I know it sounds strange and scary, but we need to do this to help your daddy."

Anneliese had been translating Cole's explanation. When she finished, Cole told Anneliese to ask Ilse if she understood and was she okay with giving Werner some of Cole's blood .

Anneleise said, " Ilse wants you to make her daddy well."

"Tell her not to look when I poke myself with the knife."

When Cole saw Ilse close her eyes, he quickly made a fast, deft stab with the knife into the cephalic vein at the wrist of his left hand. Not satisfied with the response, he stabbed again, generating a good blood flow with his second attempt. He caught the spurting blood in the mug which, unfortunately, did not look too clean, but nonetheless would suffice. He caught nearly a whole cup before he used compression to cease the flow. With Anneliese's help, he tied his handkerchief around his wrist tightly to keep the bleeding contained.

Cole had Homer and Anneliese pull Werner to a sitting position, while still keeping him mostly covered with the wool blanket.. He then had Anneliese sit next to Werner and carefully try to put small amounts of the blood from the mug into his mouth. Even in his weakened state, he reflexively swallowed the small amounts she was placing in his mouth. After a while, he tolerated larger amounts and eventually began to take good sips from the cup. After drinking half the contents of the mug, Werner opened his eyes, recognized Anneliese and smiled. Through a series of peeks, Ilse had watched the cup fill with blood and now openly watched her mother assist her father in consuming the blood. When her father turned to look at her, Ilse dashed over to him and put her arms around her father and mother.

Homer had gone forward while Werner was drinking from the mug . He was back with news from the pilot. They were making excellent time since turning Northwest towards Copenhagen due to a favorable tail wind and probably would begin their approach in not much more than half an hour. Once they were near, the pilot would use the radio to send a short, meaningless phrase that would alert the ground crew at the remote field they were using to turn on the field lights so they could safely land.

"Homer, this will be a trip to tell your grandchildren about years from now. Interesting experience aside, I hope you and your friend are being well compensated for this day's work. We are certainly grateful for your keeping us out of the hands of the bad guys. You have done more good today for more people than you will ever know," said Cole.

"The money is good but my buddy and me don't care much for those sons of bitches Nazis. We had some really good smuggling routes until those bastards came along. We always enjoy putting a kink in their tails. By the way, your friend is looking a lot better. I was kind of worried about him for a while. I would've hated to see him go south in front of his little girl and wife. Well, I'm gonna go back up and take a seat. If you need anything just call me. When we're about to land, I will holler at you."

Cole walked over to where Werner was sitting. He was leaning against Anneliese but she seemed to be managing his weight well enough. Ilse had helped her mother to give the last of the contents of Homer's mug to her father, who although weak and pale had begun to talk a little to Ilse and Anneliese.

Cole put his hand on Werner's good shoulder and bent over to whisper in his ear.

"I knew all along that this whole damn business was really just about your getting some of my blood."

Werner began to chortle, which startled Ilse into crying out "Is daddy okay?"

Cole said, "He is fine .He's just laughing."

Ilse began to giggle, then said in halting English,

"Cole, I love you. You made my daddy laugh."